Tory shivered in

Marc scared her to death. There was just so much of him.

His hair, as dark as her own, was tied back in a short ponytail, and a diamond earring flashed. His scuffed cowboy boots were set apart, his arms loose at his sides as he assessed her from her head to toe and back again. He didn't look like a spy or a mercenary. Not that she'd any idea what one looked like, but surely not like a cross between a predatory animal and an outlaw biker?

And why did he keep looking at her like *that?*

"So many books, so little time!" is both **Cherry Adair's** credo and lament. She loves to read and write—and often has a difficult time deciding which to do. Cherry began writing at the age of five, cutting pictures out of magazines and writing stories about them. When she discovered Harlequin books as a teenager, she was determined to become a writer. Along the way she also began a successful career as an interior designer, married and had children. Cherry is thrilled with the publication of her first novel, *The Mercenary*.

THE
MERCENARY
CHERRY ADAIR

Harlequin Books

TORONTO • NEW YORK • LONDON
AMSTERDAM • PARIS • SYDNEY • HAMBURG
STOCKHOLM • ATHENS • TOKYO • MILAN
MADRID • WARSAW • BUDAPEST • AUCKLAND

To Judith Duncan
for your help and staunch support
and
Elda Minger for i-dotting and t-crossing
and most of all
for David, the last of the good guys,
for always being there
THANK YOU, LOVEY

ISBN 0-373-25592-6

THE MERCENARY

Copyright © 1994 by Cherry Wilkinson.

All rights reserved. Except for use in any review, the reproduction or utilization of this work in whole or in part in any form by any electronic, mechanical or other means, now known or hereafter invented, including xerography, photocopying and recording, or in any information storage or retrieval system, is forbidden without the written permission of the publisher, Harlequin Enterprises Limited, 225 Duncan Mill Road, Don Mills, Ontario, Canada M3B 3K9.

All characters in this book have no existence outside the imagination of the author and have no relation whatsoever to anyone bearing the same name or names. They are not even distantly inspired by any individual known or unknown to the author, and all incidents are pure invention.

This edition published by arrangement with Harlequin Enterprises B. V.

® and TM are trademarks of the publisher. Trademarks indicated with ® are registered in the United States Patent and Trademark Office, the Canadian Trade Marks Office and in other countries.

Printed in U.S.A.

Prologue

THE RED BLAZER truck careened up the driveway spraying dust and gravel, spooking the cattle that grazed by the fence. *Damn.* Marc Savin's eyes narrowed with annoyance and he was tempted to walk back into the house and lock the door. He knew who his visitor was, but he wasn't ready for company even if it was a man he respected.

Alexander "Lynx" Stone, his partner and friend. Marc hadn't seen him for two years. A good guy to have at your back. But Marc didn't need Lynx at his back now. Phantom was retired. For good. Nothing Lynx could say now would bring him back.

It took everything out of a man when he was responsible for killing the woman he loved.

Marc kept his eyes on the plume of dust and took a swig of beer. With his other hand he rubbed at the scar on his shoulder. The scar and the memories were two years old. The scar didn't hurt.

The Blazer slid to a stop, and Alex unfolded his lean frame from the driver's seat. Marc watched as his friend strode up to the porch with his familiar, loose-hipped gait.

"Hey," Alex said.

"Hey, yourself," Marc replied. "Don't tell me, you were just in the neighborhood—"

"And decided to drop by," Alex finished with a grin. But Marc could see the worried expression in his green eyes. He wondered how much his friend had guessed about his self-imposed exile, then wondered why he even cared.

"Nice place," Alex commented, glancing around at the ranch house, barn and fenced-in corral. A few quarter horses grazed in the pasture beyond, while in another paddock, a prize red bull lazily swatted at flies with his tail.

"I like it. Now, would you mind telling me what the hell you're doing here?" Marc demanded, his voice heavy with disgust.

"It's Spider—"

"No."

"Goddamn it, Marc, will you listen to me—"

"Nothing you have to say is of any interest—"

"The whole damn operation is going down in flames." This was Lynx talking now—not his friend Alex. "There were three rogue agents, Marc."

That caught Marc's attention, in spite of his attempts to stay emotionally removed.

"Who?"

"Curtis, Michaels . . . and Krista."

Marc was up and off the steps before he thought about it, advancing upon his friend as a red-hot rage fired his body.

"You're a stinking liar!"

"Truth, Marc." Alex didn't back down from his rage, merely looked at him with empathy in his green eyes. "She was a double agent from the beginning—"

Marc didn't give him a chance to finish, simply connected his fist to Alex's jaw with a satisfying slam. Alex staggered back against his truck, rubbing his face ruefully. "I know how hard it is for you to believe."

"No!" The anguish in Marc's voice made it rough and harsh, even to his own ears. "No, you son of a bitch. No!" He reached over and grabbed fistfuls of Alex's shirt, pulling him away from the vehicle.

Alex expertly warded off his blows, refusing to fight back. Finally, frustration got the better of him, and he punched Marc in the stomach. Both men were experienced fighters, both had been expertly trained in the art of defense and destruction. Almost ten minutes passed before they staggered apart.

"You're being stupid, man," Alex whispered. "She turned on her country, and on you, too. She was rotten, Marc." His mouth was bleeding, and he swiped at the flow with an angry gesture.

"Shut the hell up and get off my land. And don't come back."

"Come with me to Marezzo," Alex countered. "We need you."

What Alex had told him about Krista was overwhelming him, seeping into him, making all the anger and pain and heartbreak flow back into his system as if it had all happened mere days ago instead of years.

Two years.

"They're dead, Marc. All of them."

"Shut up—"

"The royal family. The king and queen of Marezzo and their son and daughter. Executed. They didn't have a chance, with the information Spider had—"

Marc opened his mouth to say something, but found his throat had closed.

"Spider has the island, Marc. They've taken it over and God knows what they have planned. So go ahead and play cowboy if you want, but I'll be leaving tonight to stop them." Alex turned and headed toward his truck, not sparing Marc a glance.

Marc stared at his friend, rubbing his jaw. Alex still packed a hell of a punch.

He waited, hoping Lynx would simply start the damn truck and leave. Instead, his friend grabbed a thick manila envelope from the front seat and started back toward him.

"Read it and weep, you stubborn bastard." Alex threw it onto the wide porch, then turned on his heel and went back to the truck. He opened the door and got in, then rolled down his window. "And try to sleep at night, thinking about what those butchers are getting away with!"

Marc's throat tightened. He had to make Alex understand. It wasn't that he didn't want to. It wasn't that he even had a choice. He'd be useless on a mission.

"Alex." Lynx hesitated before starting the vehicle. "Alex," Marc said again. "I . . . I can't."

Something in his tone must have gotten through to his partner, because Alex looked down at his bruised knuckles grasping the steering wheel and studied them for an inordinate amount of time. When he finally spoke, his voice was gentle.

"Then tell me what the hell's going on—why have you refused missions for the last two years?"

Marc tensed. "It's no big deal. I was in the business for almost half my damn life. Half my life fighting other people's wars. I wanted out." It wasn't all a lie, but it wasn't all the truth, either. It would have to do. "Take care of yourself," Marc muttered, embarrassed by the emotion that had crept into his voice. "Don't be a god-damn fool over there."

"You've got my word on that." Alex's brilliant green eyes were so very alive. "Just promise me one thing."

"Yeah?"

"I screw up, pal, you come get me."

"Get going."

"Promise?"

"Will you leave if I do?"

"You have my word on it."

"For what that's worth. Okay, you got it, buddy."

Alex pressed his advantage: "I could do with some company."

"Get going."

Marc watched as the Blazer tore down the gravel road, spitting up small rocks and dust.

Alex would be back.

Marc sat down on the porch steps. The envelope was behind him, but he never once turned to look at it.

It took him four days before he worked up the courage to open it.

Three days after that, word came that Lynx was dead.

1

THE FEELING THAT someone was watching her woke Victoria Jones. For a moment she lay very still, her eyes closed, her heart pounding an uneven tattoo beneath her sore ribs.

The only sound was that of a log flaring in the fireplace. She could feel its heat and see the dancing orange light through her eyelids. She couldn't hear breathing but she just *knew* someone was in the room with her.

To still her panic she counted to a hundred and twenty, then opened her eyes. The library was dim, but firelight illuminated a pair of nonchalantly crossed, booted feet across the room. Tory's gritty eyes took in tight jeans and long legs. The shape of a long, lean male torso disappeared into the darkness.

Her heart was in her throat as she struggled to sit up. She hadn't meant to fall asleep, and now she was groggy and disoriented and at a distinct disadvantage.

Her hair had come loose and floated around her shoulders as she swung her feet to the floor and searched with her toes for her shoes while trying to tame her hair back into its customary bun.

Despite everything, her grandmother's strict teachings came to the fore and she said in a prim, polite voice,

"Excuse me, I must have fallen asleep." She peered across the room at the man. She felt more in control with her shoes on, and better when she was standing.

"What happened? Miss the Holiday Inn?" The man's voice was deep and rough. Tory had never heard anything so vibrantly male in her life.

"I'm sorry, I have jet lag. I didn't realize..." Tory tugged self-consciously at the hem of her jacket. "I didn't realize that you would be so long...."

"Considering that I don't know who the hell you are, nor, unless I miss my guess, did we have an appointment—"

"I'm Victoria Jones." Tory said quietly, scarlet with embarrassment.

"Very nicely said." Marc didn't add that he'd found *that* out by checking the driver's license in her purse. "Why do I feel as if we should be sipping tea while you try selling me a set of encyclopedia I don't want? I'm sorry, Miss Jones, but whatever you're selling, I'm not buying. I've had a bitch of a day. I'm cold and tired and hungry."

"Are you Marcus Savin?"

"The one and only." His tone was slightly amused as he reached over to turn on the lamp beside him.

Tory blinked into the light and squinted at him. Marc Savin wasn't anything like she'd envisioned. In a flash she noticed everything about him, as if the world had slowed its spin—a peculiar, terrifying feeling. Dread tightened her throat.

His eyes were gray, but not the soft warm gray of a kitten or the comforting gray of a favorite blanket. His eyes were the cold, icy-pale gray of the sky just before a frost, the bleak soulless gray of bare tree branches frozen for all time. Victoria shivered.

She could see dismissal coming. She straightened her spine as she stood, and stepped forward onto the thick wool Persian carpet between them, her hand outstretched.

"Mr. Savin, I'm—"

"You've already told me who you are, Miss Jones. I just don't know what you're doing here."

For a moment her hand stayed poised in midair until she realized he had no intention of touching her. Her hand dropped to her side and clutched the fabric of her skirt. Despite all the hours of rehearsal that Victoria had had on the plane, she was suddenly tongue-tied.

She knew what she must look like—an exhausted woman, with wild dark hair and wrinkled clothes. She absently touched her face where the cushion had left an indentation on her cheek and forced herself not to fuss with her clothing. Her arm throbbed. Not for a moment was she going to let him see just how terrified she was. She tilted her chin and returned his stare.

She saw the way his eyes narrowed when he noticed the cast on her arm, and everything inside her froze as he asked grimly, "How did that happen?"

"I fell."

His eyes took in the grubby cast, then scanned her face. It took every ounce of willpower she possessed for Tory not to touch any of the bruises she'd so carefully covered.

She saw a muscle clench in his jaw. "Cut the crap, lady. We can start with who did this to you."

"I told you. I fell."

There were many ways to detect a liar, even a good one. Marc didn't need to see the pupils of her enormous green eyes dilate, nor did he have to hear the way her speech accelerated. Victoria Jones was a lousy liar. He relaxed marginally.

Victoria felt the heat in her cheeks get hotter and her gaze skittered back to the pattern on the carpet before rising and fixing on his face.

"Let me put it this way, Miss Jones. I'll ask the questions. All you have to do is supply the answers. If I don't like what I hear, you'll be out of here so damned fast your head will spin. Got it? What happened to your arm?"

Tory licked her dry lips. "I was mugged at the airport."

"No husband following you?"

Hateful man. "I'm not married."

"Now why doesn't that surprise me?"

Tory tried to make her arm inconspicuous and bent to pick up her purse from where it had fallen to the floor. Her mouth was dry and she could feel perspiration beading her skin. He scared her to death. There was just . . . so much of him.

His hair, as dark as her own, was tied back in a short queue and a diamond flashed in one ear. His scuffed cowboy boots were set apart, his arms loose at his sides as he slowly slid his gaze down from her head to her toes and back again. He didn't look like a spy or a mercenary. Not that she'd had any idea what one looked like, but surely not like a cross between a predatory animal and an outlaw biker?

Obviously not impressed by what he was seeing, he said, "What can I do for you, Miss Jones? It must be something compelling, to force you to wait so long." His eyes shifted to the indented cushions on the sofa behind her and then narrowed on her face.

Victoria had never had a man look at her like that. It was disconcerting. Glancing outside she saw that night had fallen while she slept. The wind sounded mournful as it whipped the bare tree branches and rattled the window. She shivered. Jerking her gaze away from the night sky, she turned back to him and said, "I need your help."

"Why should I help you?" Marc asked over his shoulder as he strolled over to the built-in bar across the room to pour himself a drink. "I've never seen you before in my life."

Victoria licked her dry lips. "May I have a drink, too, please?"

"Sure. What'll it be?"

"Whatever you're having." Her fingers actually hurt from clutching the handle of her purse so tightly. She deliberately relaxed her hands as she walked over to the French doors and rested her hand on the heavy, navy blue velvet draperies that framed the window.

It had started snowing. The snow looked pretty, soft, white. But snow was another unknown. She shivered. Already unnerved by too many weeks of the scary and the unfamiliar, Tory gritted her teeth and turned back into the room.

It was warmed by the blazing fire in the hearth, which caused reflections of dancing amber light from the highly polished dark wood floor and the smooth surfaces of the two dark blue leather sofas that flanked it. Wall-to-wall mahogany bookcases rose to twelve-foot ceilings. Victoria trailed one hand across the tempting bookbindings before casting an anxious glance at the man across the room.

Having counted all the books on the left-hand wall after she'd arrived hours ago, she was about to start on the right when he silently came up behind her. Tory almost jumped out of her skin as he handed her a glass.

Marcus Savin was nothing like she'd expected. For one thing, he was young. Well, not young, but in his mid- to late thirties, which was twenty years younger than she'd anticipated. If his hair had been loose, it would probably touch his broad shoulders. He was wearing stone-washed jeans and a cream-colored fisherman's-knit sweater and looked like someone that had stepped out of the pages of a magazine. *What the well-dressed predatory male wore.* Victoria blinked at her own imagination.

She accepted the glass from him and took a long drink. It was cold and wet and for an instant felt great going down—until it burned like fire.

He stood watching as she gasped for breath. The whiskey fumes made her eyes water and her throat close up. Savin's face was impassive. It took every ounce of her control not to cough. But she did it. She shot a poisonous glare at his back as he walked across the room.

"Next time, ask for water."

"Next time *offer* me water."

Marc dropped down on the leather sofa opposite her. His drink balanced precariously on his flat stomach, he settled one arm behind his head and stared her down. Her eyes slid away and then back. Her arrogant little nose tilted.

"You know my brother." She moved cautiously to the other end of the sofa and sat on the very edge, pulling her skirt down over her knees. When she leaned forward to put her glass on the coffee table, she exposed the vulnerable ridge of her collarbone below the lacy edge of her collar. "Alex—Alexander Stone."

He narrowed his eyes fractionally. "I don't know anyone by that name. Sorry honey. Try again."

"Lynx," she said tightly. "You *do* know Lynx. You sent him on a mission to Marezzo seven months ago." She straightened and stared at him. "I'm his sister." Her jaw tightened and something flashed in her green eyes. "And don't say you don't know him. *He* told me all about *you*." Marc just stared at her.

"I know, for example—" Victoria kept her eyes fixed on a point behind his left ear "—that the organization you work for is an elite unit. A cloaked counterterrorist force beyond even the CIA. A highly secret group called T-FLAC. Terrorist Force Logistical Assault Command." She licked her bottom lip. "I know there are members of your team infiltrated into all sorts of foreign governments and military organizations all over the world."

A small triumphant smile curved her mouth as his shoulders tensed. The next moment he was up off the sofa and had her upper arms in a punishing grip. She hadn't even seen him put down his glass. Her shoulders brushed her ears and Victoria gave a little yip of distress as his fingers tightened until she was on tiptoe. His eyes bored into hers like burning ice.

"Who the hell are you, lady?"

She tried, God help her, she really tried, to say her name, but Victoria was so terrified her lips barely moved. Her eyes darted about the room, looking for help; but of course they were alone. She suddenly realized with a sinking heart that other than Marc Savin's people, no one knew she was here. He could do anything to her and probably would. He shook her and Tory's teeth chattered. "My brother—"

"Would sure as hell not turn rogue and give away so much information dead or alive. Try again, green eyes." He shook her again. "I'll give you about two seconds to tell me who sent you, and then—"

"Your code name is Phantom," Victoria said quickly, her skin going hot, then cold and clammy. "Oh, my goodness. Would you please stop shaking me like this? I'm going to be sick on your carpet!" His hands abruptly loosened. Victoria quickly moved behind the sofa, smoothing her jacket down with a shaking hand. "My brother is alive and *not* well in Marezzo, Mr. Macho Spy Master. So it won't matter one bit if you shake me or torture me. *That's* still a fact. The only reason I know all this is because—"

"He didn't have any relatives."

"Try again, Mr. Savin. I'm standing right here before your very eyes. I'm Alex's twin sister and I'm very much here." Her hand bunched her hair and he could see the tension in her body. "And don't talk about him in the past tense. Alex is *alive*."

Damn, was it possible? Was it even conceivable that Lynx was alive? Of course the canny Lynx would have kept a sister under wraps. He was normally a closed-mouthed bastard and would have known Victoria would be an easy target for anyone with a grudge. Then again, she could be anybody.

"How do I know you're his sister?"

"Don't be ridiculous! Why would I be here if I wasn't?" she shot back, and her green eyes, so much like her brother's, flashed again. She moved around the barricade of the sofa. "He has a birthmark on his right hip shaped like a half-moon." She obviously didn't realize how much she exposed as she furiously pulled up her skirt to bare a pale slender thigh. A pink birthmark, shaped like a half-moon, marred the smooth skin under her panty hose.

"It's a moot point, isn't it?" Marc retorted, deceptively relaxed. "He died while he was on vacation, I believe." And if the son of a bitch wasn't dead, he would be when Marc found him. He thought of what he'd been through in the last six months. Only Lynx could have blown their cover like this. Marc's mind was racing with the ramifications of Lynx's betrayal. Had Lynx come to the ranch to lure Savage into a trap?

"He was *captured* while he was on a *mission*," she insisted. "You sent him there and you had better get him out."

"I saw his body seven months ago."

She flinched. "I beg your pardon, but I saw him *alive* two weeks ago. You sent him to Marezzo and he's still there." Marc saw the muscles work in her throat. "He's been imprisoned for almost seven months. They— they've tortured him."

She lifted huge green eyes to his, and Marc found himself drawn into their anguished depths. He cursed under his breath. It wasn't possible. He'd seen the body. It had been burned beyond recognition, but the dental records . . . Hell, it had been Lynx. He was sure of it. Damn, but he was sick of this business. Every time he got close to someone, he lost them. Lynx had been the last straw. He was too damn old for all this shit.

His head shot up as he suddenly realized what she'd said. His eyes narrowed. "What the hell do you mean, you *saw* him?"

My God, could it be true? Had this idiotic woman actually gone to Marezzo and found her brother? Had she done what a team of crack agents should have done?

"I went there to find him."

Marc closed his eyes, squeezing the bridge of his nose. He opened his eyes and cast her a dubious look before saying slowly, "Marezzo isn't exactly a vacation paradise, honey. That's the home base of a nasty little group of terrorists, known as Spider. You can't just go waltzing into their nest as if you were taking a little holiday!" His blood ran cold at the thought of a civilian on that volatile little island in the Tyrrhenian Sea. "Terrorists took control of the island. Tourists are merely tolerated as a front, and I know damn well that going over there with a broken arm like a little lame bird wouldn't even get a sympathetic glance. They'd kill you quite happily if you so much as looked like you were going to interfere. These are big bad people, green eyes, and Marezzo is no place for little Miss Muffet."

Marc thought that her face drained of color but she seemed to straighten her spine as she said flatly, "What I saw of it was quite pretty, actually."

"What you—! Are you out of your mind, woman?"

"I can see why tourism has gone down. I had my wallet stolen twice." At first he thought she might be joking, but when he looked at her, he saw that she was quite serious.

She was ticked off because her wallet had been lifted! "You're damn lucky it was only your wallet!" The dying fire bathed her face in a rosy glow that made her look a whole lot more appealing.

But not to him, of course. Her type of woman drove him nuts. Her naiveté irritated. He wished to God she'd cover her thighs. Her skin was ivory pale and looked silky and just too damned touchable.

He looked pointedly from her face to her legs and back again. She jumped as if he'd used a cattle prod, jerking the skirt down as far as she could. Her face turned scarlet.

"How old are you, for Christ's sake?"

"Twenty-si— What has my age got to do with anything?"

There wasn't enough damn room. He needed to be outside, under the open sky. He glanced out the window and saw it had started to snow. *Great. Just great.* It suited his mood perfectly. He paced between the sofa and the door, the door and the sofa. Ending up in front of the fireplace, he tossed in a log and turned to glare at her. "So, you want me to go and get him, is that it?"

Her chin rose. "You were the one who sent him there. It's only fair."

"Lady, nothing in this world has ever been fair. Your brother was—"

"*Is!*"

"*If,*" he continued without pause, "he was alive, I can assure you that I'd know it."

"You didn't," she countered reasonably. She rose and came to stand beside him. The fire added some much-needed color to her face. She tilted her head back to look up at him. Marc felt the shock of her small hand on his arm right through his thick sweater.

"They have him on the southwest side of the island, near a little fishing village called Pescarna. He's in really bad . . ." She swallowed hard, her eyes suddenly awash with tears. "They've hurt him. Badly. He—he didn't even recognize me." Tears leaked down her cheeks and her fingers tightened on his arm.

"Please. Help me."

"No."

For a moment there was silence as Victoria stared up at him. "No? You're saying *no?* Despite the fact that you sent my brother to Marezzo, you won't go in and rescue him?" Her jaw ached with fury and frustration.

Marc Savin leaned an elbow against the oak mantel, looking as relaxed as a cat. "It's nice to know you have such a good command of the English language, Miss Jones. You got it in one. Your brother is a good agent, and like all good agents, he knows the odds."

"But you thought he was dead. Now that you know that he isn't—"

"It makes absolutely no difference, Miss Jones. I haven't anyone to spare right now, and even if I did—"

"What kind of man are you? They're *torturing* my brother. How can you just stand there so complacently and pretend not to care?"

One moment he was completely relaxed, the next he was right in her face.

A tidal wave of panic threatened to overwhelm her. Her knees locked and her insides were crawling, the muscles in her stomach constricting as if she could at least draw that small part of herself away from the overwhelming menace of him.

His breath was hot on her face when he said grimly, "This ranch is the only thing that keeps me marginally sane and reminds me I'm still part of the human race, Miss Jones. Just because your brother gave you my name does *not* give you the right to barge into my home and demand anything. Got that?"

He was so close, Tory could see the pale squint lines beside his eyes and smell the faint scent of soap on his skin. The fiery heat of his body, so close to hers, made her dizzy. She flinched, her trembling fingers touching her throat as he looked down at her, his eyes narrowed and hard.

When she remained mute he said softly, "I have spent almost half my life in hell so that people like you can sleep safe and sound in their beds at night. I'm just not interested at this late stage in saving a damsel in distress, whatever her problem. In the beginning I felt what I was doing made a difference. Now, I'm too damn jaded to care one way or the other."

"You heartless son of a—I can't believe that anyone could be so unfeeling! Alex thinks of you as a friend."

"In this business I don't have any friends."

"Goodness gracious, I can certainly see why!"

Marc watched the emerald sparks in her eyes. He felt more alive than he had felt in thirty months.

Tory tried to moisten her dry lips. She felt the wild thundering of her pulse and swallowed hard. Her eyes focused on the plaid wallpaper and for several seconds she counted the horizontal lines before she turned back to face him, her mouth set.

"That leaves me with two choices, then."

"I can assure you, I don't want to know."

"One, I can go back and try to find him by myself...."

Marc laughed. "Get real, lady! You said you've already been to Marezzo. If you could have gotten him out, you wouldn't be here now."

"Two," she continued as if he hadn't spoken. "I can go in to town and talk to the nice people at the local newspaper." She looked at him with guileless eyes.

"There *is* a newspaper in Brandon, isn't there? I'm sure they'd love to have the scoop. Do the townspeople have any idea you're a mercenary?"

Tory had heard the threat coming out of her mouth— she just couldn't believe she'd actually had the guts to say it. Her hands were damp as he stepped in front of her.

Well over six foot, he towered over her. His unshaven jaw was taut with fury in a face that was too masculine, too hard to ever be handsome. His nose was an aristocratic slash between dark brows that were drawn inward. The unseasonable tan on his face had an underlying gray cast as he glared at her out of colorless eyes.

His lips were a thin tight line and a muscle jumped in his cheek as he stopped a hairbreadth in front of her. Tory swallowed sickly and she tried to back up.

The diamond earring glittered as he lifted her chin with his finger and lowered his head until they were almost eye to eye. "You," he accused, "must be either very brave or very stupid, Miss Jones."

Tory gulped. If he didn't know then, she had no intention of telling him. Her eyes felt bone dry as she forced herself to hold his gaze.

Still tilting her face up he said flatly, "No one knows that you are here, do they, Miss Jones?" Before she could even formulate a reply he continued. "Did it ever occur to that agile little brain of yours that you might know just too damn much?" His fingers tightened around her jaw. "That if I am who you *think* I am, I can't let you leave here?"

Tory's skin stretched painfully across her cheek-bones. Her body was paralyzed as he held her gaze. "No one would know if you disappeared from the face of the earth, now would they, Miss Jones? So if the 'local newspaper' needed a story, and someone just *happened* to find a mutilated body down by the river— Oh, for God's sake, don't faint!"

He caught her awkwardly as her eyes rolled and she slumped forward. The cast on her arm banged into the coal scuttle and he winced as he swung her up in his arms and strode over to the sofa, where he dropped her none too gently. When she didn't open her eyes he tossed a blanket over her legs, moved the arm in the cast out of the way, and started undoing the little pearl buttons of her blouse.

His words had only partially been a bluff. Victoria Jones knew more than was good for her. Marc frowned.

Her skin was silky smooth and warm against the backs of his fingers and instead of stopping when he reached her plain white cotton bra, Marc continued to ease open the blouse until he came to the skirt's waistband, where he had no choice but to stop. He grinned when he saw the bra—white cotton with not a hint of cleavage. The only reason he'd opened her blouse was so she could breathe. Pulling the blouse together in deference to maintain her modesty, Marc picked up the glass of whiskey she'd set on the table.

Crouching down beside her, he forced the glass between her lips. Her lids fluttered and then she fixed her big green eyes on his face and opened her mouth like a baby bird. There was no choking this time, as she took dainty sips of whiskey.

"You're very literal, aren't you?" He absently wiped a drop of amber liquid off her bottom lip with his thumb. She stared up at him, unblinking, as he rose and set the empty glass back on the table.

"Actually," she said in a small voice, "I'm pretty much of a coward."

Marc's tone was dry. "You could have fooled me."

"Really?" She looked ridiculously pleased as she gingerly swung her legs to the floor, feeling around for her shoes. When she couldn't find them she settled one foot on top of the other. "Well, I might be a chicken but I don't usually faint like that. Sorry." Then she fiddled with her hair until Marc said, "Leave it!" Her hands dropped to the blanket in her lap.

Refilling his glass, he quietly watched her. The silence built and built and he could tell by the stiffness of her shoulders that she was ready to break, which was fine with him. He would give her directions to the Motel Six in the next town and be ecstatic to see the back of her.

Her chin wobbled.

Marc ground his teeth.

A single tear welled and ran down the side of her nose; another one followed.

Marc scowled. The fact that she didn't utter a sound made the tears more poignant. He jammed his fingers into the back pockets of his jeans and glared into the leaping flames. In his mind's eye he saw her shoulders heaving, but when he turned to look, she was as still as a statue. Her lips were moving in a silent litany, which Marc realized was counting. It sure as hell wasn't helping him, and he was up to two thousand eighty-six.

He drew in a deep breath and aimed for five thousand.

The lines on the plaid paper blurred as Tory continued to stare at the wall. She didn't know what else she could say, what else she could do to convince Marc Savin to go and get Alex and bring him home to her.

"He's—" There was a catch in her voice as she turned to face him. Her soft, pale mouth trembled as she whispered helplessly, "He's all I have. Please. I'll do anything you want. *Please*, help me."

Marc felt the ice around his heart melt a little. He looked down at her glossy head. When he didn't answer she wiped the tears off her face and turned to look out the window, obviously trying to compose herself. Her back was ramrod straight.

Dammit, didn't she realize that her blouse was undone? His eyes were drawn to the slender wedge of pale skin he could see reflected in the window—skin that looked so soft and smooth and . . . defenseless. Marc squeezed the bridge of his nose.

"Put that blanket around you or do up your blouse," he said, more gruffly than he'd have liked as he forced himself to concentrate on her face. "Tell me everything."

Flushing, Victoria did up her blouse and pulled the blanket around her shoulders. She turned an eager face to him. Her bare legs were still uncovered, but he could deal with that. She had good legs—long and slender, with incredibly delicate ankles. Luckily he'd always been a "breast man" so her legs didn't have much effect on him. Not much.

She sank back with a wince and blew a breath upward to clear a tendril of hair from her eyes. Covered to her knees by the mohair blanket, she looked like an orphan rescued from a storm. With every movement she made, more and more hair slithered loose from the coil at the back of her head.

"Where do you want me to start?"

Marc came and sat on the coffee table, facing her. Their knees were almost touching. "Start at the beginning and don't stop until I tell you."

"I have, or I had," she corrected, "a condo in San Diego. I always kept a room for Alex. He'd come once in a while and stay for a few days in between . . . assignments. Not as often as I liked, but he did stay a few times a year." She shrugged out of the blanket and he saw the pink mark where it had scratched her throat. The blanket settled around her hips as she fiddled with her hair. She used the waist-length strands like worry beads and Marc absently filed that information away.

"He used to send me a letter—mailed to a post-office box in Mission Valley—before each assignment. I was to keep it until he came and got it. I'd pick up the letter, take it home and wait for him. He'd come back and burn the letter. I never read any of the letters—not until the last one."

"What made this time different?" He leaned over and tugged at the blanket until it covered her knees to his satisfaction. Surprised, she looked at him, then continued softly: "He always gave me a time frame. Ninety days. I was supposed to wait for ninety days after he was due back, before I opened it. A week after he was due back I had this awful feeling—I just knew that something had gone drastically wrong...."

"What made you think he wouldn't be back?" Marc asked. "He'd been back late from assignments before. These things never run on a fixed timetable."

"We have a . . . connection." She looked him straight in the eye. "A telepathic connection, if you will."

Marc couldn't negate what she'd said. He'd seen some amazing things while he'd been in the field. "So you packed your bags and went off on a little vacation to look for him. Is that what he told you to do in the letter?"

She flushed. "He told me where his last assignment was and told me to contact you if he wasn't back by the end of the month. And I didn't go on a 'little vacation.' I called you. You were gone. Indefinitely, they said. I couldn't wait. Alex was being hurt, and he was calling me. I went."

"Calling you? How?"

"I don't expect you to understand." She looked grim as she said urgently, "I *knew* he was in trouble. I had absolutely no idea when or *if* you would be back. For all I knew, you were with him."

Marc winced.

"I sold my condo and some other investments. I had no way of knowing how long it would take to get him out. I wanted all my resources liquid. Then I flew to

Rome and from there I rented a boat and went to Marezzo."

Marc got up and started pacing again. "So you waltzed in and asked someone where your brother was."

"Nobody asked me anything. I looked like a tourist. The pickpockets treated me like a tourist. I carried a camera and I did some sight-seeing. And I did find Alex. Which," she said hotly, "is more than I can say *you* did."

Marc felt his temper flare. She was annoying as hell. But she was right. His people had shipped Alex Stone home. He'd done a cursory inspection and believed Lynx was in that body bag. He grabbed the phone, punched a series of numbers, and waited. After rapping out a string of numbers, he held the line again. Victoria sat stiffly, her face devoid of expression as she listened to his short commands.

"We have a code five on Marezzo. Who've we got? Yeah, lousy timing. I'll be coming myself. I'll take care at this end. I'll leave the transportation and ordinance to you." He looked at her assessingly and frowned. "I'm bringing someone with me. A woman. Expect us tomorrow at 0900."

"Surely you didn't mean . . ." Victoria went white. "Oh, no! I can't go with you."

"I don't have a choice." Marc slammed down the phone and resumed his pacing. "You're the one that can communicate with Lynx. If you're not with me, I might not be able to find him."

"Of course you will." She sounded panicked. "You're a spy. You do this kind of thing all the time. It's your *job*. You don't need me to slow you down." She held up her arm. "I have a broken arm. I can't go running around chasing the bad guys."

Marc crouched in front of her and took her chin in his hand. "Lady, that's your brother over there. If I say I need you, I need you. If I say go, you go. If I say jump, you ask how high. Got that?" He felt her teeth grinding together under his fingers and saw her pupils dilate as she swallowed convulsively.

"I . . . I'm a coward. Okay? I don't do well under pressure. I'm a bookkeeper, for goodness' sake. Not Mata Hari. I used to work for an auto-parts store because I don't even like the pressure of tax time."

"You know what Will Rogers said—'We can't all be heroes—someone has to sit on the curb and clap as we go by.'"

"I can clap for you from here."

"You're going."

"I could wait for you in Rome," she begged desperately.

"You're coming with me to Marezzo."

"I'll fall apart," Tory said, catching his wrist and staring up at him with pleading eyes. "Oh, please. Believe me. Taking me with you will be the worst mistake. I'll draw you a map of where they're holding Alex. You'll have no problem finding it. Really. Give me a pen and I'll show you—"

"Listen to me," Marc said slowly. "The last thing I want to do is haul your butt over there. But I don't seem to have a choice. You are going to Marezzo. For all we know, they've moved Lynx and I'll never find him without you."

He did not say that she was his insurance. If she was anything like Krista, he would give her no opportunity to set him up. Victoria Jones was going to be right by his side whether she wanted to be or not. He gave her a cold look. "Unless you were bullshitting me about this telepathy bit?"

"No, that's the truth." Her shoulders slumped. "Don't say I didn't warn you, though, when I cower instead of attacking."

"Nobody will be attacking anybody. We go in, find Alex, and get the hell out." He'd get the job done. In, out. Clean and simple.

"Don't say I didn't try to warn you," Victoria said weakly. "I just know you'll be sorry."

2

MARC WAS SORRY. Sorry that he'd forced her to go and sorrier still that they were in this stinking fishing boat from hell.

He was sorry she'd spent the first three hours puking her guts out over the side of the boat. He wanted to join her. The waves crashed into the side of the forty-foot hunk of wood until he was sure they'd have to swim the next hundred miles. Salt spray shot twenty feet in the air and soaked everything in sight. He'd tried to keep her down in the relative warmth of the cabin, but the smell of fish had been so overpowering, even he hadn't been able to stomach it.

Tory dry-heaved over the side. Her stomach hurt, her arm throbbed, and she hated Marc Savin more with each passing moment.

The man was relentless. Well, she'd warned him. That gave her a little tingle of satisfaction.

"This really gives you a thrill, doesn't it, you bastard." At the sound of Marc's voice, Tory raised her head weakly from the railing and glared at him. But he wasn't talking to her. He was smiling that hateful smile and talking to the fisherman who was steering this death trap out to the open sea. Her head flopped back as her stomach heaved again.

"*Certo!*" Angelo exclaimed with gusto, the muscles in his massive arms bulging with the strain of controlling the wheel. "Look at those waves, my friend. It makes us remember who is boss, no?"

Marc glanced up at the dark sky. A bright moon shone down and illuminated the glistening deck. To the east he saw a thick bank of clouds moving swiftly toward them. "It makes me think you've used this damn cover too long."

He glanced over at Victoria, who was waiting for a merciful death. "Time I got you back in the field, Angelo. You're having just too damned much fun. How soon till we get there?"

Angelo looked down at the waterproof watch on his massive wrist. "It's O2300. The storm will cover you when we land. You're going to have to swim the last couple of hundred feet to the beach. You sure she'll make it?"

"She'll make it if I make it," Marc said grimly and went over to make sure the plastic bag he'd wrapped around her cast was still watertight. He handed her the canteen and told her to rinse her mouth out.

Gulping the water, Victoria shot him a furious look when he took it away and handed her a stick of gum.

"I don't chew gum," she said primly. "It isn't ladylike."

"It isn't exactly ladylike to puke your guts out, either." Marc unwrapped it and stuck it in her mouth. "Chew."

She glared at him out of bleary eyes. "Remind me never to go out on a date with you ever again." Her jaw worked the gum. The flavor of mint bursting on her tongue was a blessing.

Marc suppressed a grin. "Remind me never to ask you on a date ever again. Can you make it another forty minutes?"

"What's the alternative?"

He pushed her dripping hair out of her eyes and laughed. "You could always swim."

"How far is it?" She looked serious. An enormous wave broke against the side and she let out a little shriek as hundreds of gallons of water crashed over them. Marc held on to the rail and pulled her against his chest as the wave foamed at their feet.

The wind whipped her hair into his face. It smelled of baby shampoo. "That was close." He tightened his arms around her narrow waist, burying his nose in the wet, fragrant mass.

Her voice, muffled by his yellow slicker, vibrated against his chest. "I don't even like this kind of adventure in a *movie*. I can't remember what it's like to be dry." Her bright eyes peered up at him. "And I think I swallowed my gum." Marc chuckled and she pushed at his chest. "How come you're having so much fun, anyway?"

Another wave crashed on deck a few feet away and he used it as an excuse to pull her closer. She fit rather well against him, despite the bulky slicker encasing her. "Oh, we spies just live for adventure." The corners of his mouth tilted in a reluctant grin.

Marc saw the pulse beat in her throat. Her dark lashes were spiky, her long hair slicked back, exposing a bruise and a bump on her forehead. She'd regained a little color and her lips were a pale petal pink.

My God, he thought in amazement. *She's gorgeous*.

She was still staring up at him, her arms wrapped around his waist as he dropped his mouth to hers.

She tasted delicious—of mint and sea salt—as he ran his tongue across the seam of her lips.

"Open your mouth for me."

"I don't think that's ..."

Marc slid his hand up under her soaking-wet hair and held her head in his palm. "Good idea, don't think. This is in the way of an experiment." He took her mouth again, plundering the hot wet interior as another wave crashed down beside them. He felt the sharp edge of her teeth and pressed closer, cursing the bulky slickers that kept him from feeling her soft curves against him. She whimpered low in her throat as he rubbed against her, but she didn't pull away; instead he felt her slight body sway into his.

Tory's arm came up instinctively to pull him closer. She wished she had the use of both arms. He tasted marvelous. Exciting. Thrilling. She gave herself up to his devouring mouth.

When the next wave poured over them she held on tighter, her mouth still fused to his as salt water ran down her neck and sheeted their faces. His kiss was like nothing she'd ever experienced before—hot and dark and totally unpredictable. His tongue demanded that she respond. And she did—wholeheartedly.

"Hey, you two!" It took a moment for Tory to realize where she was, and she flushed, pulling away as Angelo shouted again. "Land ho!"

As Marc let her go, Tory looked over the side of the heaving boat. "Land ho—where?" All she could see in any direction were mountains of churning gray water beneath hills of black clouds.

She gripped the slick railing with one hand as Marc and Angelo gathered their things together. Angelo helped Marc shrug into the A.L.I.C.E. pack and then handed him several mysteriously wrapped packages, which Marc tucked into his belt.

He stripped off the slicker and bundled it into another pouch clipped to his belt. His jeans were black with water and the heavy cable-knit sweater sagged as he slipped off his shoes and used the laces to tie those to his belt, too.

Tory gave him a wary look as he made his way barefoot across the tilted deck toward her. Her lips still throbbed from that kiss. She could almost imagine her heated mouth hissing as water drenched her from head to toe.

"Now you, princess. Off with that slicker." He started unbuttoning it and Tory tried to bat his hands away. She spat her hair out of her mouth as the wind lashed it around her.

"I'll be soaked."

Stripping off the slicker, Marc stuffed it in with his own.

"Now your shoes." The wind and rain cut straight through Tory's thick sweater and leggings and froze her to the marrow as she struggled with the laces, eventually handing her shoes over. When he didn't answer her, Tory said with a giant shiver, "I don't have to tell you why I prefer dating accountants. They never make me do things like this."

Marc checked his supplies one last time before glancing over at her. "I'll keep that in mind. Let's go."

"Go where?" She looked around for a dingy. "Oh, no! Oh, no, oh, no!"

"Hold your breath, sweet pea. Here we go." Marc took her hand and pulled her over the railing.

She'd no idea which end was up. The pressure of the black water came at her from all sides. *Don't panic, don't panic.* Water filled her nose and she panicked. Arms and legs flailing, Victoria swallowed a mouthful of salt water as her body's natural buoyancy turned her right side up, bobbing her to the surface.

She gagged, treading water as best she could. She didn't want to think of what a tasty meal her bare pink toes would make for some creature of the deep. Her right arm was useless. The best she could do was try to float it in the plastic bag. Okay, so she could swim for it—wherever "it" was.

Everything looked the same metallic gray as her eyes scanned the water for Marc. She just had a cast on her arm to worry about. Marc was loaded down with equipment.

A few seconds later she was underwater again, her hair in her face.

Her heart was pounding double time as she bobbed once more to the surface and then felt something grab her sweater from behind. She let out a gargled, blood-curdling scream.

"Have a...heart...honey. If I'd wanted them to...know...we were coming I'd have sent a... telegram."

Tory was too exhausted and too relieved to see him to talk. She relaxed marginally as he started towing her—hopefully, toward dry land. Kicking her legs and using her good arm, she tried to help. He used the swells to propel them through the surf to the beach.

Sand scored her stomach as the water pushed them farther up the beach. For a moment she simply lay there with her face pressed to terra firma, the waves hungrily sucking at her quivering legs.

"Time to go." Marc staggered to his feet, pushing his dripping hair out of his face and pulling her up beside him. For one horrible moment Tory didn't think her legs would work as they both reeled unsteadily. Marc's arm came out to support her, bumping her hip with whatever it was that heroes wore around the waist.

The moon played hide-and-seek with the clouds, illuminating the hard planes of his face only sporadically. It started to rain. Victoria sighed.

"I hope we're checking into a Hilton. I'd kill for a hot bath and a cup of tea." The rain poured down in a torrent, and she licked her lips. The water was sweet. Looking up to the black sky, she let the water sluice over her face and tripped over a large dead tree limb. Marc used her own momentum to keep hauling her on. She glanced around curiously. It was pretty hard to see anything in the dark. The ocean gave off a faint phosphorescence and all she could see was beach stretching out in front of them. Up ahead was the solid, paler gray outline of a cliff.

She tugged on his hand and he stopped. She could just make out a feral gleam in his eyes. "I hope you don't think I'm going to climb that cliff. Because I've got to tell you—"

She caught the faint flicker of his smile. "We're checking into the Hotel Grotta Zaffiro."

"Oh, please," Tory said fervently, "don't be joking." She felt him tug her hand as they made their way to the base of the cliffs. It was rockier here and her bare feet came into contact with hard stone instead of hard-packed sand.

"In twenty minutes you'll be up to your pretty neck in hot water," he promised.

Tory grinned. It sounded like heaven and gave her a new burst of energy as she scrabbled over a big boulder.

They seemed to be climbing, but it wasn't straight up. Piles of large rocks and boulders littered the base of the cliffs and they had to pick their way carefully in the dark. That hot bath was sounding better and better all the time.

Surely they would have to find a road soon. The rain had stopped and the sky had lightened to pewter as they climbed. Marc hadn't said a word for ages when he turned to give her a hand up.

She was out of breath and panting as she dropped her hand to her knee and hung her head to gulp for air. Her hair pooled on the rocky ground in stringy skeins. When she straightened, Marc was grinning.

"What!"

"You look like Medusa." He laughed softly as she gave a horrified gasp, her hand going to her snarled and tangled hair. Taking her hand he pulled her after him. "Actually, all things considered, you look damn good. Come on, princess, your bath is waiting."

"I hope this hotel is at least a two-star— Oh, Marc, no. Please, tell me we aren't going into a cave."

"We aren't going into a cave," he said agreeably, his fingers tightening on hers as he pulled her toward a small hole in the face of the cliff.

She saw the narrow beam of light pool at his bare feet as he turned on a flashlight, turning it so that she could find her footing behind him.

It took a moment for Tory's eyes to adjust. "You rat, you said I'd have a hot bath." She followed behind him closely, looking anxiously about the narrow cavern. "There'd better not be any bats in here."

"No bats."

The cave smelled damp and unpleasant, but that was par for this course, Tory thought crossly. Trust him to promise a hot bath just to get her moving. They walked straight ahead for a while, then turned a corner and went straight again. Then they went down a slope, walking for what felt like at least another mile.

She stumbled over a protruding rock, stubbing her toe, and then had to scurry behind him as he forged ahead. She took his hand gratefully when he stopped to wait for her.

"Okay?" His voice bounced off the narrow walls, his fingers were warm as they closed more tightly over hers and he moved forward again.

"Oh, I'm just peachy." Tory lowered her voice as she heard how nervous she sounded in the echo. "What happens if this path runs out and there's nothing up ahead?"

"If I fall down a black hole, just let go of my hand. Someone's sure to rescue you if you go back down to the beach."

Tory's footsteps slowed at the thought that they might end up at the bottom of some deep dark hole, never to be heard from again. She shivered in her wet clothes, holding on to his hand like a lifeline as she moved close enough to his back to feel the heat of his body.

The thin beam of the flashlight illuminated only a few feet in front of him. The cramped walls of the cave closed in around her, the rough surface of the rock snagging on her sweater.

Marc said into the silence, "I've been here before, green eyes. There are no holes to fall into. Don't worry."

Easy for him to say! Tory stuck as close as she could without tripping them both.

Her bare feet hurt, as did a hundred other spots on her poor, unheroic body. She wanted to complain but didn't want to give him the satisfaction of knowing that she really was a wimp.

Tory bit her lip as they were suddenly plunged into darkness when Marc clicked off the flashlight. "Close your eyes."

Tory was only too glad to comply. The darkness was oppressive. "Can I lie down while I do it?"

"No." She could hear the smile in his voice as he urged her on. "Keep those eyes closed. You're going to like this."

Tory kept her eyes closed but she muttered grimly under her breath, "If it's going to be another scenario where you're the hero and I'm the shivering coward—"

"Open your eyes, princess."

Slowly Tory slitted her eyes open, then stared with eyes and mouth wide. "Marc . . ."

They were standing in an enormous cavern. The ceiling was a hundred feet or more above their heads. The entire area was filled with a shimmering iridescent turquoise light that made everything look somewhat unreal. In the center of the giant natural auditorium lay a placid lake. Mist floated above its surface and draped over the lush emerald ground-cover and ferns at the water's edge.

"Oh, Marc." Victoria was utterly speechless. She'd never seen anything quite so beautiful in her life.

"Grotta Zaffiro," Marc murmured reverently. "The Sapphire Grotto."

Marc saw her shiver and cursed. Victoria had to be exhausted, and her broken arm must hurt like hell. He'd dragged her halfway around the world and tossed her into a stormy sea. She needed food and rest before they could go on.

"You can take in the sights later." Marc propelled her toward the back of the cavern. "Let's find a relatively safe place to bed down and then you can take that hot bath."

"I thought that was just an inducement to get me here."

Marc heard the exhausted slur of her words and kept a steadying hand on her arm. "There's a hot mineral-spring pool about three hundred yards back." His own body quivered from exhaustion, and *he* was trained for this. For all her protestations of being a coward, she'd done amazingly well. But now, her face was colorless and her lips tinged with blue.

Stopping abruptly, Marc let her sink to the sandy floor. "Rest here for a moment while I go and check out our room."

She immediately curled into a ball and closed her eyes. "Call me when room service gets here...."

Marc scouted the enormous cave for a safe place to bed down. Marezzo hadn't had many tourists since it had become the playground of the terrorists. But still, he didn't want to take unnecessary risks in case some adventurous resident should bring guests to see the natural springs and grandeur of the grotto.

There was only one entrance—the one facing the sea in the limestone cliffs. He walked deeper, the sapphire glow of the water fading. The faint odor of sulfur assaulted his nose as he came across the small pool of steaming water. The underground spring that fed it was several hundred feet away, so the water was pleasantly hot and the smell of sulfur not too overpowering.

That hot water was going to do them both a world of good, once he'd found somewhere to stash their things.

The small space he was looking for was well hidden by a sixty-foot wall of solid limestone—a natural room of about a hundred square feet, tucked away and undetectable.

Dropping his supplies on the sandy floor, Marc began making a rough camp. Setting up a small propane stove, he poured bottled water into a tin pot and set it to boil before going back for his reluctant partner.

She was exactly as he'd left her—curled into a small ball, her wet hair trailing in the sand.

"Room service."

She didn't move so much as an eyelash. Picking her up, Marc made his way back to their "room." She was out like a light. Briefly he debated waking her so that she could take a hot bath and change into dry clothes. But she needed sleep now more than creature comforts.

Stripping naked out of his own soaked clothes, Marc turned down the flame on the stove and then dried off with the clean T-shirt he found in his pack.

Digging a depression in the sand, he laid down a foil survival blanket and turned to Victoria. Her mouth was slightly open. She'd be pissed as hell if she knew she snored. Gathering her hair in both hands, he squeezed out as much salt water as he could, then efficiently braided it to get it out of the way. Pausing with his fingers in her hair, he took stock of what the hell he was doing. Suddenly he was coldly furious with himself, realizing that somehow she'd managed to bring out a new and unfamiliar tenderness in him. In his line of work it was dangerous to be distracted. He pulled the thong out of his own hair and tied it around the end of Victoria's.

She was trouble with a capital *T*. He didn't need to know her to realize that the very correct Miss Victoria Jones was going to be a pain in the butt. That kiss on Angelo's fishing tub was an indication that he was slipping.

She wasn't his type. She was the type of woman who wore her blouse buttoned to the throat and her clothing like armor. Hell, she probably wore support hose with her medium-heeled shoes.

He liked to see a woman look like a woman. Slinky clothes and stilettos. He'd always preferred women who knew the score and accepted a one-night stand. Quick, satisfying sex with no commitment. That used to be his style. Now, with God only knows what diseases going around, it was becoming more trouble than it was worth.

Perhaps the fact that he'd been celibate for more than three years had something to do with it. Impatient with the way his thoughts were going, he pulled the wet leggings down her legs. Her flesh was bumpy from the cold. And bruised.

Marc leaned back on his heels, frowning. What in the hell was this? His eyes quickly cataloged the marks on her smooth skin. The bruises were purple and ugly. He swore viciously under his breath as his finger touched first one, then another, and then another. The bruising was not random. It was precise and systematic.

He had no idea just how long ago she'd been beaten. But there was no doubt that Victoria Jones had survived a vicious and brutal beating by an expert.

Stripping off the waterlogged sweater and skimpy bra, he checked out the rest of her body. Most of the marks were contained between her shoulders and knees. He frowned.

He used a T-shirt to dry her clammy skin, which was silky smooth as he ran the fabric over her face. The bruise on her forehead had already started to fade to a sickly yellow.

He forced himself to concentrate on a few inches of skin at a time. The fact that she slept through his ministrations indicated just how exhausted she was. If she woke up now, she would probably bring the roof down. His grin died as he trailed the warm damp cloth over her breasts.

Small, plump, perfect breasts.

Her pale nipples peaked as the soft fabric moved across skin. Marc finished, then carried her, naked, to the makeshift bed. She was so deeply asleep she didn't stir when he pulled a clean, dry T-shirt over her head. Covering her with another blanket, Marc first checked that the plastic had kept the cast dry and was relieved to see only a little moisture had seeped in the top. When he was sure she was as comfortable as he could make her, he grabbed a small bar of soap from the pack and went to the natural hot spring, where he sank up to his neck in the steaming water.

VICTORIA AWOKE FROM a dream with a start, terror making her heart pound as she sat up. She squeezed her eyes tightly.

Alex, oh, Alex, where are you? We're here. We'll find you. Just tell me where you are!

The only sound was that of her pounding heart. She tried to open her mind and concentrate, but thoughts kept crowding in and she was aware of nothing but her own fear.

Frustrated, she opened her eyes to an eery blue glow, then inhaled the mouth-watering savory smell of stew. Her stomach growled. At least there was one body part that was in working order.

She felt a violent surge of panic when she realized she was alone. She glanced at the gently simmering pot at the entrance to the "room." Marc couldn't have gone far if he'd left something cooking. Scrambling out of the warm cocoon of blankets, Tory realized she was naked beneath a knee-length black T-shirt, and she flushed hotly. *Blast that man!*

Finding his backpack, she took out underwear and a dry pair of leggings, which she pulled on under the shirt.

Feeling more comfortable now that she was decently covered, Tory prowled around the camp. She saw signs that Marc had dug himself in for the long haul. A large inflatable water bottle was filled and propped against the back wall next to what looked like a radio. He'd used a ledge in the rock face as a shelf for other supplies. Absently she folded the wet clothes he'd tossed in the sand, making a mental note to wash them.

The bed he'd fashioned was for two. Well, if he'd slept there with her she didn't remember it. The last rational thought she'd had was how incredibly beautiful the cavern was.

She was dying to venture out and have another good look at the beautiful expanse of fresh water, and perhaps take a swim. Her skin felt sticky, and her hair was stiff with salt and sand.

The savory smell of the stew drew her to the pot. It looked as good as it smelled, activating her salivary glands and making her stomach rumble. Tory couldn't wait. For all she knew, Marc would be gone for hours. She picked up one of the forks and stabbed it into a piece of the meat.

She made herself stop eating when she realized she'd finished half of the stew while crouching down beside the little propane stove. She hadn't even bothered to ladle it onto a plate. Obviously, adventure was turning her into a savage.

There wasn't much to do other than fold the top thermal blanket. After that was done, Tory laid it with perfect precision on the end of the "bed." She didn't want to think of lying there with Marc Savin for who-knew-how-many hours, wearing nothing but his shirt.

Folding her legs, she settled herself against the cool rock to wait for him. When she heard something on the other side of the rock wall she froze, then quickly scooted on her bottom into the back where the shadows were deeper.

Fool. The first thing she should have done when she woke was find some kind of weapon in that black bag of his. There was another scraping sound from the other side of the rock. Her eyes darted to the black pack sitting uselessly next to the water bottle five feet away.

Someone was out there, and the smell of food would bring them right to her. Her hands started to sweat as she heard the sound of a heavy tread dragging across the sand-strewn rocks out of sight. There was a pause, then the footsteps came closer.

Tory inched against the wall toward Marc's black pack. It was probably full of all sorts of violent things. It didn't matter that she would have no idea how to use whatever she found. Hopefully, it was something big and dangerous looking.

Keeping her eyes firmly fixed into the light, she reached out, her fingers touching the thin plastic skin of the pack. Holding her breath, she felt for the catch and flipped open the top. The metal ring clinked against stone. Her blood froze as the footsteps beyond her vision paused and then kept coming.

She felt something soft and pushed it impatiently aside as her hand rummaged again. Her fingers encountered something hard this time. Hard and cold and mercifully heavy. Almost choking, she forced herself to take nice deep breaths as she hefted the weight in her left hand and raised it over her head.

"I hope to hell you know what to do with that thing." Marc Savin's words cut into her terror and her arm dropped. "Usually one shoots with it, but I suppose an exception can be made in your case."

He looked like a modern-day pirate in his dark pants and shirt, his black hair loose and skimming his broad shoulders. He also looked annoyingly clean and alert, while she felt rumpled and out of sorts.

Tory glanced down at the nasty-looking gun still clutched in her hand. She was holding it by the barrel. She jerked her hand away, dropping the weapon, and rose to her feet. "You scared me to death! Why didn't you call out or something?"

Marc poured what was left of the stew into his plate. "I thought you'd still be sleeping." Folding his legs, he sat down and dug into his meal. "Put the Uzi away and find the coffeepot."

Tory filled the battered pot from the water bottle and turned up the flame on the stove. He told her where to find the coffee, then leaned his elbows on his knees.

"How are you feeling?" he asked her.

"Better than I should," Tory admitted, pouring the grounds into the container. When the coffee was ready, she filled the two cups he held, then settled down to sip the hot fragrant brew. "What time is it, anyway?"

"After three. You slept for twelve hours straight."

"I wish you had wakened me." Tory clasped the warm cup between her hands, settling the container on her drawn-up knees. "I had a dream last night." Her dark braid fell over her shoulder and she set the cup down on the sand, fiddling with the dark tip of hair. Then she raised her head and looked at him. "Alex is badly hurt, Marc. He's almost dead. I can feel it." She gazed over his shoulder without focusing, swallowing hard.

In her dream, Alex's face had been beaten so badly it was totally unrecognizable. The dream had left her shaken and frightened to death that they might be too late.

"I'll go in after dark and bring him out." She saw how his lips tightened and she picked up her cup, draining the last drop. Her mouth was suddenly bone dry.

"I did a quick reconnoiter this morning in Pescarna. If that's where they are holding Lynx, then they're doing a damn good job of covering their tracks. It will save hours of time if you can pinpoint exactly where he is." Marc swallowed the last of his coffee and poured the rest of the pot into his cup. "Whatever his condition, I'll get him out. Angelo will be waiting for my signal."

She didn't like the way Marc said, "whatever his condition." Her throat was tight when she spoke. "How long do we have to wait before we can find him?"

"I hate like hell having to take you at all. All I want you to do is tell me exactly where he is. Then I'll bring you back here." He tossed her a towel and a small bar of soap. "If you turn left and go about a hundred feet you'll find your hot bath. Take your time and let the water get out some of those kinks." He pulled her to her feet. "I'll be at the main entrance, keeping a lookout."

Tory set her cup next to his on a rock ledge. "To tell the truth, I'd be more excited if you told me there was a bathroom around here." Flushing, she picked up the wet, folded clothes, adding them to the soap and towel.

"Your every wish is my command, princess. Follow me."

The cavern was about the size of two football fields, the walls pale in the eery glow. The sapphire water was crystal clear, casting shimmering waves on the walls.

Tory walked beside Marc as they circled the lake on the far side. "How do all these plants live in here?" she asked as they passed a shrub covered with tiny white flowers. Ferns and moss grew right to the water's edge.

"There's plenty of natural light and fresh water." Marc plucked one of the flowers and stuck it in her braid. "Let me know if you want to swim, though. The water here is over forty-five feet deep. Its clarity is deceptive." Circling around a huge fern that was as tall as he was, he turned back to look at her. "See that whirlpool at the end?"

In this light, with the reflection from the lake, his eyes were crystal clear and looked blue. "What is it?"

"That, princess, is a natural drain." He pointed back the way they'd come. "The hot spring is back there in the gut of the mountain. The water pools in the depression near camp and then runs into this lake. By then it's cold. The water drains down a forty-foot tunnel directly into the sea below. Don't swim here unless I'm with you. That drain hole is wide enough to suck you right down to the rocks below."

Tory shivered. She'd had enough of deep water yesterday when he'd dragged her overboard.

He pointed out three Porta Potti toilets standing sentinel discreetly around the corner from the entrance. "Only the one on the left still works. They were stuck in here for the tourists, but there haven't been any visitors to the grotto in years."

"Why not? The cavern is the most beautiful thing I've ever seen."

"Remember the rocks we climbed to get here yesterday? Those crashed down from the cliffs. It isn't safe for tourists at the moment. Besides, since the terrorists claimed Marezzo back in 1987, they've discouraged tourism to a certain extent. A few tour groups are allowed in every now and then to preserve their cover. But it's pretty much their island. The locals are all basically keeping a conspiracy of silence. Their lives and livelihoods depend on it." Marc pulled the Walther, from the small of his back and double-checked it, ignoring the way Victoria's mouth pursed at the sight of the weapon.

"I'll be just outside if you need me. The hot spring is back the way we came."

THE POOL WAS ABOUT six feet across and surrounded by water-smoothed rock. The bottom was a powdery sand. Tory stepped into the hot water, making sure her cast stayed dry. The heat felt wonderful as she sank in up to her chin, her hair floating around her. Sighing deeply as her aching muscles relaxed in the warm water, she closed her eyes against the steam.

"What in the hell do you think you're doing?"

Tory shrieked as she blinked her eyes open to see Marc Savin emerge through the steam. Water splashed over the side of the pool as she slithered upright, her hand to her throat.

"What are you doing here?" she gasped. She'd fallen asleep and it took a moment for her brain to kick into gear. Her cheeks flamed as his cold gaze drifted down to where her wet hair clung to her bare skin.

"What the hell's taking you so long?"

One arm was useless as a cover. Tory quickly whipped the towel off the rocks and into the water and slapped it over her chest: her knees made little islands above the water as she drew them up to cover as much of herself as she could. "I must have fallen asleep. Look, I'll just finish up here and . . . Would you please leave." Mortification made her voice choked. She flushed from her hair to her toes.

He came closer. Tory licked her lips and slid farther under the water with the wet towel clasped to her chest. "Please. Just *go*." She was afraid to blink, thinking that he was already too close.

He was wearing jeans, but he hadn't bothered to button them. His naked chest was darkly tanned, a thick trail of crisp black hair ran in a vee from his chest down into the open fly. He crouched down beside the pool, his knees spread for balance. Flushing even more, Tory rippled her gaze away from what was now at eye level. If she'd reached out her hand she could have touched him, he was so close.

Her heart rose to her throat. She didn't know where to look—there was so much of him. The movement had opened his fly that much wider, but he didn't seem to notice. He was tanned all the way down. Tory stifled a whimper.

Steam moved in lazy swirls around his head. His hair was loose, hanging to his shoulders in a dark shiny drift that was disconcerting.

She stared at a distant point on the other side of the cave. The wet terry across her chest felt heavy, forcing her to take deeper breaths. She could feel his stare like fingers sliding down her naked skin, and she shivered.

Managing to look him in the eye she said in a small voice, "Please. Will you just go away?"

Marc stared down at the woman in the water. The steam shimmered on her pink skin. It looked as smooth and soft as a baby's. Her wet hair effectively blanketed her body, trailing in the clear water like seaweed.

Her knees were drawn up to her chest, and her feet were one on top of the other as she tried to hide her body under the dubious protection of the clear water. A fragrant blob of soapsuds slid down her silky shoulder, and dropped to float on top of the water by her hip. He knew he should leave. It was absolutely crazy to have come looking for her in the first place.

Even the center part in her hair was pink with embarrassment.

"We'll be leaving at first light," he said briskly, shifting to his feet. Her face went even redder as he turned back to look at her.

"Fine," she managed, eyeing him warily. He could see the frantic pulse in her throat. Christ. He was going to have a hell of a time with her. She was such a little mouse. She quivered if he even looked at her.

"I'll get you a dry towel." He glanced at the wet material molded to her breasts as she shifted restlessly.

"Thank you," she said stiffly.

Perversely, Marc stayed. "You sound like a prim little schoolgirl," he said mockingly. "Can't you say anything other than 'Thank you'?"

Her head tilted regally. "Yes. I can say *go away!*"

"Green eyes, there's nothing here that would make me want to stay." The way she tilted that chin irritated the hell out of him. He wanted to see just how far he would have to push her for her to fight back. He sighed. It was a useless endeavor. She hadn't been kidding when she'd said she was a coward.

"I hate you," she said in her quiet little voice, looking at anything but him.

"Say it louder."

Her eyes shot back to his face. "Wh-what?"

"Say it louder and with feeling. Let me see *how much* you hate me."

"You're crazy!"

Without being aware of it, Marc took the three steps required to reach her side again. He crouched down and took her quivering chin in his hand. Her eyes were wide and frightened. "Let me see some grit and backbone, lady. I'm already having second thoughts about hauling your ass to Marezzo."

"I told you I didn't want to come."

"Yeah, you did," he said roughly. He dropped his hand from the damp heat of her face and levered himself to his feet. "I'd feel a little more confident if you showed some spunk."

"You want spunk?" Her eyes blazed. "How's this for spunk?" Whipping the soaking towel off her chest, she threw it at him with all her strength.

The soaking fabric flopped down harmlessly into the sand. Her eyes shot emerald sparks at him, and her jaw was rigid. "I'm here on Marezzo with you, Mr. Marc 'Phantom' Savin. I'm here, but I don't like it." Her voice rose. "I don't like it and I *certainly* don't like you." She threw the soap next; it glanced off a button on his fly and dropped behind a fern.

"I'll give you *spunk!*" She picked up a small smooth stone, throwing that, too. Marc grinned as it missed his head by two feet. "Atta girl!"

"You are a *loathsome* man."

"Yeah?" Marc smiled. There was hope for her yet.

"Yes! Stop taunting me . . . and go . . . away!"

"Or what?"

Victoria looked at him. He was cocky and arrogant and just too blasted sure of himself. She'd read about men like this. She might need him to find Alex, but that didn't mean that she had to like him. She stared at his insolent face. She needed to establish right now that she wasn't just going to take everything he dished out. But how?

He loomed over her, bare feet spread, arms folded over his naked chest, jeans unbuttoned with casual disdain for her embarrassment. He was doing it on purpose, too; she knew that. He knew that she was rattled and he was having a fine old time at her expense.

What could she do that would rattle *his* cage . . . ?

Before she could really think the action all the way through, Tory rose from the water. Keeping her gaze fixed at a point to the left and behind Marc, she stepped onto the rocks on the rim and then moved around him. Water sluiced down her goose-bumped skin. Every nerve in her body was mortified, but she kept her back straight and her head high as she walked past him.

Her face burned, but not for anything in the world would she let him see how shaken she was and how much courage it had taken for her to get out of that pool naked.

She felt totally exposed and more vulnerable than she had in her life. But she wouldn't back down. Mingled with her mortification was the sudden realization of what guts it had taken.

Oh, my God, she thought incredulously as she heard his startled gasp behind her. *I did it!* Her spine rigid, Tory forced her footsteps to stay even and refused to give in to the temptation to run and cover herself. There was no sound from behind her, but she would have been hard-pressed to hear anything over the thundering of her heart. She was five steps from the entrance to the camp when a hard hand gripped her upper arm. She screamed.

Marc swung her around to face him. There was a nasty glitter in his pale eyes as he held her chin tightly between his fingers. "Listen to me well, princess. Sex doesn't mean a damn thing to me. Got that? So don't throw that delectable little body in front of me anymore, because I'm just not buying."

Without a blink, Tory stood frozen in his grasp. His lips were a hard thin line and his eyes were narrowed on her face. Inwardly she flinched at the iciness of his expression and her heart pounded. What a nasty excuse for a human being he was.

"How dare you! I wasn't throw—"

"Get real, lady. I've been around the block a few times. Let me put it this way: I'd be tempted if I didn't consider sex right up there with other dangerous habits like drugs and drunk driving. You look clean, baby... but these days, who knows?"

The blood drained from her face, then heat washed over her from head to toe in a blind rage. Without thought, her arm swung up and she hit him so hard across the face that he had to take a step back.

"Little bitch," he said mildly, as she spun on one dainty foot and marched into the alcoved camp. If there had been a door, it would have slammed. A wise man would have given her a few moments to cool down.

"The slap was warranted." Marc said as he followed right behind her and headed for the stove to pour a cup of coffee. "Just be warned. Next time, I'll hit back."

"Next time you insult me like that, I'll use a gun and you won't be in any condition to retaliate one way or the other." Victoria's voice was rock calm.

She was sitting in the middle of the makeshift bed, cradling her arm, wet hair soaking the shirt she'd pulled on over her damp naked body. She wasn't giving an inch. From the little he knew of her, he was astounded that she'd dredged up the nerve to pull that little stunt. His eyes narrowed in speculation.

He'd known before they started out that she'd be a pain in the ass. But damn it, he needed her to find her brother. He didn't have a choice. On the other hand, he mused with great annoyance, he hadn't given her any choice, either. Luckily, what he'd told her had been the absolute truth. Sex was more trouble than it was worth, these days. He had enough danger in his life from his job. He'd eliminated all his bad habits over the years so that he could focus on staying alive.

The coffee in the metal cup was cold. Marc drank it anyway, irritated as she gave a little sniff. Oh, great. Back to her usual modus operandi. Marc didn't acknowledge the relief he felt. Victoria Jones, the wimp, he could handle.

He crouched down beside her. His soap smelled completely different on her skin. "What happened? Does something hurt?" When she didn't respond, he lifted her chin to look into her face.

"Are you sick? Does your arm hurt? Are you embarrassed that I saw you naked? What?"

He saw that her eyes were filled with tears. *Great!* "Talk to me." His voice came out a little harsher than it should have.

"Leave me alone." Her voice was soggy as she jerked her head away. His fingers tightened on that stubborn little chin, and she glared at him, the tears making her green eyes glitter. "I broke the comb. Okay? I broke the blasted comb!"

Marc stared at her as if she'd lost her mind. "You're crying because you broke a damn comb? Christ, lady, it's a fine day when that's the worst thing that can happen to you."

He got to his feet impatiently, paced to the back of the cave and pulled out the radiophone. If she was going to freak out over something as ridiculous as a broken comb, they were in big trouble.

She pushed her hair aside and looked over her shoulder. "What are . . . are you doing?"

"Calling Angelo. He can come and get you the hell off this island." Marc punched out the code again on the mobile phone. *Damn fool woman.*

"No!" Tory jumped up. "No, don't do that. You need me to find Alex. You said so."

"Lady, I must have been out of my ever-loving mind to think you'd be any help. Look at you. You're already falling apart and we haven't even got to the hard part yet."

"You don't understand." She bit her lip as Marc glared at her. "I can't do my hair," she said simply, her head dropping and the fall of wet silk blanketing her body.

He'd known her for little more than a day and in that short time he had her figured. She was a lousy liar, which he liked. She was too damned sexy without being aware of it, which he *didn't* like. He might not know her well, but one thing he did know was that she was obsessive about being neat.

Marc remembered the prissy, navy blue suit and sensible pumps she'd worn when he'd first met her. He'd a sudden mental image of her straightening her collar and striving to neaten her hair when she first woke up.

He suddenly saw her in a completely different light. Her bare feet were sandy, the T-shirt she wore was crumpled from being in the pack, and her hair was wildly tangled.

"Come here," he said gently.

3

WITH A HAND ON HER shoulder, he pushed her down on the blanket and settled cross-legged behind her. "Give me the comb."

"I don't want you to touch me, thank you very much."

"I don't want to be kept up all damn night because you're sniveling about your frigging hair! Give me the comb!"

She handed a piece of the broken comb to him over her shoulder.

"Relax." He picked up the towel and rubbed at her hair.

Her voice sounded muffled and sheepish. "My grandmother used to do that."

He rubbed out as much of the moisture as he could, then picked up the comb. Her hair pooled on the silver blanket between them, and he picked up the ends and started drawing the teeth through the wet tangle.

"Tell me about her," he said softly, trying to distract her. Her hair felt like silk.

"My father was a stuntman, and my grandmother hated that. She thought my mother should have married a doctor or something. His work was so dangerous. My mother used to go with him on his gigs. She liked all the traveling. They used to leave us...leave us with my grandmother when they went off. When we were six they didn't come back."

Marc smoothed her hair across his knee. "What happened?"

"They were killed while Dad was filming in Spain. Their plane crashed. My grandmother kept me. She sent Alex to a foster home." Her shoulders hitched. "We hated that. He went from home to home. He could never be adopted—Grandmother wouldn't allow it. She adopted me. But she wouldn't adopt Alex."

That explained the different surnames. It also explained how Lynx had managed to keep a twin sister under wraps. Grandmother sounded like a royal bitch. Marc felt a swell of compassion for her, which annoyed the hell out of him. He frowned. He didn't have time for that kind of emotion on a mission. His senses had to be razor sharp or they were all going to end up dead.

"We could sort of communicate, but we didn't see each other again for almost eight years. I hated it," she said fiercely, and Marc felt the tension in her back. He kept combing.

"I did everything right so that she would bring Alex home. She wanted a nice, quiet, neat little girl. And that's what I was. She was my only security, and I wanted to do everything right so she wouldn't s-send me away, too."

Marc heard the tears in her voice. He could imagine that little girl. Neat, quiet and waiting for her brother to come home. No wonder she was so fanatically neat and tidy. No wonder she didn't like her quiet little world turned upside down. She'd had enough of that as a child.

Her hair was tangle free and almost dry, but Marc kept running the broken comb through it. God, she had the most incredible hair. It spilled into his lap like silk.

"When we were eighteen, Alex disappeared."

Marc knew where he'd gone. He'd recruited Alex Stone right off the street when the boy had been well on his way to becoming an accomplished car thief.

"My grandmother got sick. I nursed her till she died. Then I took the money she left me and bought a condo—" her voice hardened "—with *two* bedrooms. And I made a home for us... Alex and me." She twisted to look at him. "That was my revenge. I could make a home for us. And I did, using her money."

But it had been too late for Alex Stone, Marc thought grimly. By then he was "Lynx." And that had left his sister out—again. He forced himself to section off three heavy ropes of her hair. She handed him the tie over her shoulder when he'd finished the braid.

"Thank you." She twisted to face him. "You *are* going to find Alexander, aren't you, Marc?"

Her hair had soaked her T-shirt. The thin wet cotton lovingly accented the sweet plump curves of her breasts as she looked up at him.

"Don't worry, I'll find him." Marc resisted pushing the long silky bangs out of her eyes. "By this time tomorrow the two of you will be living it up in Rome."

Her eyes glowed. "Really?"

He'd felt the first unwelcome stirring of desire for her on the boat. But a kiss was no big deal. And, okay, he had seen her naked. Again, no big deal. He'd certainly seen more than his fair share of naked women.

At first he'd dismissed the attraction, thinking it was because of her hair. Then he'd managed to convince himself, while soaking in the hot spring, that he was in full control of his bodily urges.

He'd been dead wrong.

"Thank you." Her lips were pale, her teeth very white as she gave him a shy smile.

Using both thumbs, Marc brushed away the tears drying on her cheeks, then cupped her face. He shouldn't do this, he knew. The operation was already well on its way to being a screw-up.

He kissed her damp eyelids, and she made a murmuring protest as his fingers tangled in her hair, pushing gently so that she fell backward, half on the blanket and half on the sand.

He just wanted another small taste of her, that was all. One small taste. He settled his mouth over hers. She tasted of toothpaste, minty and fresh. He slanted his mouth and her lips opened under his. Just a little. Just enough so he could slide his tongue between her teeth. God, it was sweet heaven.

It shouldn't have been this good. As she tentatively, shyly, touched her tongue to his, Marc thought he would jump out of his skin. He forced his hands to stay in her hair. He wanted to strip her naked and drive into her with a force that rocked him. Tearing his mouth away from hers, he sat up, running his fingers around the back of his neck until he could control his ragged breathing.

She lay there watching him with those big slumberous green eyes, her lips wet and swollen from his kiss, her breathing as unsteady as his own.

"This was one bad idea, princess. Roll over and get a little more shut-eye before we go."

TORY WOKE TO DARKNESS and the single glow of the propane stove. Marc was a shadow in the shadows in his dark clothes, his expression closed. "You have time to eat before we go."

He sounded like a stranger.

Tory self-consciously ran her hand over her eyes, grateful he couldn't see her flush. "I'm not hungry."

"You'll eat anyway." He rose and dished up her meal, bringing it over to her. Tory pulled the thin blanket to her chest. She wished with all her heart that she was wearing a bra.

"Honey, I've seen everything you've got. So just drop the blanket and eat. It'll take us at least forty minutes to get to Pescarna and it's after eleven now." He pushed a fork into her hand, his eyes cold. "I hope to God you aren't expecting a big declaration. It was only a kiss. I don't plan on analyzing every damned body function between now and when we leave."

She looked up at him. "Thanks for putting that into perspective." She cocked her head and her braid slithered over one shoulder. "If I'd known I'd be reduced to a 'body function' I wouldn't have bothered kissing you back," she snapped. Setting the full plate aside, she tossed off the blanket and rose.

His jaw tightened as he gritted his teeth. She must have caught the feral gleam in his eyes for she said sweetly, "All you had to do was say no."

"Hell, you didn't even know what you were offering."

Victoria tilted her chin at him. "I don't remember my offering you anything."

"How's it feel to be the last American virgin, honey?" Marc asked sarcastically, wanting her to get angry and slug him, in which case he'd grab her and— *You've lost your mind Phantom. Get a grip on your damned hormones. This is like a jackal taunting a kitten.*

Her nose turned pink. "It feels quite comfortable, thank you."

Marc took the sucker punch like a man. He'd been joking! "I thought the definition of a virgin was an ugly thirteen-year-old."

Victoria gave him a dirty look. "I *was* an ugly thirteen-year-old. I'm also a realistic twenty-six-year-old. I like my life just the way it is, thank you very much. I didn't ask you to maul me, and I don't appreciate being taunted just because I have principles. My virginity is my business, and I'll thank you to keep your sweaty hands off me."

"Princess, sex *is* a sweaty business. I bet if you loosened up a little it would grow on you. Close your eyes and imagine two sweaty bodies rubbing against each other...."

"Why do you insist on talking to me like this?" Tory's eyes flashed. "I know you don't like me. Fine, the feeling is absolutely mutual. You were the one who dragged me here, remember?"

"Wow. You're really scaring me to death," he said mockingly, stalking her across the sand.

Tory stood her ground as he came toward her. She pulled the Uzi out of his pack—right side up. It looked ridiculous in her small hands.

He stepped right up to her so that the cool metal poked him in the chest. "Don't ever point a weapon at a person unless you mean it," he rasped. His hand shot out and gripped her wrist like a vise.

Tory's hand turned into a fist as she tried to jerk her arm away.

"I mean it."

Her lips trembled and tears welled.

Marc took the Uzi away from her and set it on top of the pack. He sighed, then put his arms around her and rubbed her back. "I'm a real bastard."

She pressed her wet nose into the vee of his shirt. "Yes, you are." Her cast bumping his back reminded him of just what a son of a bitch he was.

Her face looked pale and vulnerable in the dim light as she moved away from him. "We're going to have to cover that cast. People will be able to see it a mile away. Here." He tossed her a long-sleeved black sweatshirt.

A virgin! Didn't that about beat the hell out of everything!

She quickly pulled the thick sweatshirt over her head, muffling her voice as she asked, "What happened to my shoes?"

Marc tossed her a pair of black running shoes. "Make sure none of that white shows." He pointed, and she pulled the sleeve down over her cast.

In the process of stuffing her yard-long hank of hair down the back of the sweatshirt, Marc demanded flatly, "Are you sure you can handle this?"

"I'll do whatever it takes to get Alex away from here." She hid her terror because, God help her, the very last place she wanted to go right now was back to Pescarna.

A FULL MOON LIT THEIR way down the rocks to the beach. Because it was high tide they kept as close as they could to the base of the limestone cliffs. The full moon painted ribbons of silver on the dark water and reflected off the white limestone. The scene was like a dramatic black-and-white photograph.

The warm air was thick with the salty smell of the ocean, and the night was quiet except for the crashing of waves against the rocks and the hissing as water washed up in foamy patterns on the wet sand.

"When we get into Pescarna, all I want you to do is locate Lynx—Alex, and then I'll bring you back to camp. I'll do the rest. Got that?" He took her hand to help her over the slippery boulders.

Tory grunted. It was harder going than she'd imagined. Marc was like a cat as he jumped from one huge rock to another. She knew that she was slowing him down. But she was terrified of slipping into the wildly foaming surf that churned among the rocks. The clean, fresh scent of the sea was heady in the warm still air as she stumbled after him.

He'd told her that Pescarna was only four miles up the coast. It felt a lot farther. She almost ran into Marc's back because she wasn't concentrating. "What?"

He put his hand over her mouth. "Shh," he whispered, his fingers caressing her cheek. "We're here." His eyes glittered in the moonlight. "Which way do we go?"

Tory closed her eyes and forced her mind to clear.

Alex?

She could hear the pounding of the waves behind them and in the distance the faint sound of someone singing. Every now and then a fine mist of ocean spray reached them, beading on their clothes.

Alex? Alex. Alex. Alex!

"Hey." She felt Marc's arm come around her. "Hey!" He pulled her into the circle of his strong arms and pressed her face to his damp sweater. He smelled like the sea. "Relax, you're hyperventilating."

"Oh, God, Marc. I can't sense his presence at all."

She felt the soothing pressure of his hand rubbing up and down her back. "Just relax, honey, and open your mind. If Lynx is around he'll know we're here. Just close your eyes and concentrate."

Try as she might, Tory didn't get any response to her desperate mental pleas. She shuddered, her arms around Marc's waist tightening. "There's nothing," she said in a small voice. "Nothing." She looked up into his face. "I have to be closer. If Alex is badly hurt he might not be able to communicate this far."

"Damn. How close?"

"I won't know until I find him."

Marc brushed the bangs out of her eyes. "Promise that you won't do anything stupid?"

Tory smiled. "I'm a coward, remember?"

"Yeah. I remember." Marc took her hand and drew her over the next series of rocks. His voice was pitched low as he said urgently, "You do everything I tell you, understand? And for God's sake, stay with me."

"Yes, sir!"

Sand gave way to scrub grass and the lights of Pescarna twinkled against the night sky. Then she felt the reassuring solidity of cobblestones under her feet. She followed Marc into the shadow of an overhanging wrought-iron balcony. The spicy smell of geraniums permeated the air. The street was narrow and the cobblestones bit into the soles of her shoes as Tory clutched Marc's hand and continued on behind him.

Straining to hear him as he murmured, "We're going to just keep moving until you get something. So tell me when to stop."

Soon whitewashed Moorish-style houses rose like cliffs on either side of them. There were no people in the streets this late at night, but they could hear loud voices coming through the open windows. A canary chirped, and dishes rattled.

Blood-red geraniums spilled over balconies, and the aroma of garlic and tomato filled the warm night. The sweatshirt was too hot, but it covered the white of her cast. She concentrated all her thoughts on Alex.

An hour passed and then another. They slipped up one narrow alleyway and down another, pausing often for Tory to concentrate. Nothing. She wanted to cry, but one look at Marc's stony expression froze the tears.

The fishing village was small, but by the time they had traversed every street and alley twice, Tory was beyond tears. They emerged on the far side of the village and stood hidden in the shadow of a small grove of olive trees.

Clouds whispered across the moon. Everything was still. A dog barked, then it, too, fell silent. Tory rested her head against the gnarled trunk of a tree. "I'm sorry."

Marc longed to comfort her, but he, too, was frustrated. "We'll go back to camp and I'll have Angelo come and get you." He put a heavy arm around her slumped shoulders. "Come on. I think you've had enough for one night."

They circled the village, keeping to the shadows on the beach. The smell of fish was overpowering as they passed the dark shapes of the fishing boats. Tory tripped over a net, her eyes blinded with tears. "I felt him for a moment and then it was gone." She looked up at Marc. "They've taken him somewhere else."

"What?" Marc's voice was urgent. "*You felt him?* Why the hell didn't you say something? Where? Can you find the place again?"

Tory resisted as Marc pulled her back the way they had come. "Wait. I told you. He's not there anymore. They took him—Marc!"

"Just show me where they took him *from*. It might give us a clue where he is now."

Tory's heart skipped a beat. "It was in the house next to that trattoria. The pink house with the canary in the window."

"Let's go."

They had taken the canary inside. But Tory found the house. Three narrow stories rose above the cobbled street. The windows were dark. Everything was quiet.

"What now?" Victoria whispered, her heart pounding. The feeling that Alex had been here was strong. He'd been here recently—very recently. She shivered, her hand clutching Marc's tightly. "They took him away within the last six or eight hours. No more."

"Time for you to go home, princess." The words were merely a breath in the still, fragrant night air.

"No," Tory whispered, just as quietly. "Alex was here. There might be a clue inside."

"You'll never find it." His fingers tightened on her arm as he tried to draw her away.

"Why not?"

"Because, you stubborn woman, you are not going into that house!" he shot back under his breath.

A window down the street slid open and a man stuck out his head. *"Zitto! Se ne vada!"*

Tory froze. "What did he say?"

"He wants us to get the hell out of Dodge. Let's go."

They kept deep in shadow until they reached the end of the street. Tory stopped and tugged on his hand. "There's a back way, down this alley. Come on."

She saw Marc's eyes light up suspiciously. "How do you know there's a back way. Don't tell me you're psychic, as well."

She stepped over a pile of refuse from the trattoria, still dragging him along. "You don't want to know." They stopped under a small cement balcony.

Marc grabbed her shoulder and spun her around. "I sure as hell *do* want to know. Look at me." He held her chin. "Look at me, Victoria. That's better. There's something stinking in Denmark and I want to know what it is."

"It's that pile of— Ow!"

"Start talking, princess, and make it quick." A muscle twitched in his cheek as his fingers pinned her in place.

"I—I had the dubious pleasure of being a guest in this house for a while."

Marc looked up at the star-studded sky. "Please tell me she's joking." He looked back into her upturned face. He knew, damn it. But he didn't want to hear the answer. When he'd first met her he hadn't cared enough to pursue the issue, now he wished he had. She had the frigging broken arm. A mugging, for God's sake! Yeah, it was a mugging, all right. A professional beating by Spider henchmen. She was lucky to be alive. "When?"

"Just before I went to Brandon to find you. I was going to tell you but it didn't seem relevant."

"Didn't seem . . . relevant? Good Lord, Victoria. Of course, it was relevant." He started pushing her down the alley and didn't stop until they were back in the small olive grove. He spoke in his normal tone—furious.

"Start at the beginning and keep going."

Tory cleared a spot on the ground with her shoe and then sank down to sit crossed-legged on the dirt. "I told you that I came to look for Alex." Her troubled eyes met his and Marc forced himself to remain calm. He sank down beside her, keeping enough distance between them so that he wasn't tempted to strangle her.

"I spent a week playing tourist in Pavina. Alex wasn't there. I rented a Vespa scooter and came to this side of the island. I knew he was close, so I checked into a *pensione*." She shivered, although the sweatshirt was clinging uncomfortably to her sweaty back. "I guess I . . . I guess I asked one too many questions."

"Shit, Victoria!"

"You swear too much."

"It beats the alternative."

"Which is what?" she asked huffily, her face a pure oval in the moonlight.

"Just get on with the story."

"Two men came and told me that they had some questions. They weren't very polite about it, and they scared me to death. I said no, thank you, I was on vacation. Then they got . . . nasty."

Marc growled low in his throat like a rabid dog. *Damn fool woman!* "What did they do to you?"

"They took me to the pink house and asked me what I was doing here poking around. I kept telling them that I was just here on vacation, and they were not being very hospitable about it. I wished I spoke a little Italian. They were yelling and screaming and waving their hands about."

"Cut to the chase."

"Yes, well, that went on for a while, and then they locked me in a room upstairs and they told me to think about it. Which I did." Victoria's eyes went unfocused. "They came back and I stuck to my story and the big one in the expensive suit hit me...and the other one got mad and hit *him*. And they were yelling and screaming again. And then a man came and they...they tied me.... And then I started screaming...." She picked an olive off the ground, grimacing when she bit into it. She spat it neatly in her hand, then buried the soggy pieces in a hole she made in the dirt. "I don't want to talk about it anymore."

His jaw ached from clenching his teeth. "How long did they hold you?"

"Thirteen days, seven hours and eighteen minutes."

"How did you get out?"

"I convinced them I was telling the truth. Besides, they knew that I had to see a doctor about my arm— they took me to the airport and sent me to Naples."

It didn't make sense. Why would they keep her for almost two weeks and then let her go? "Stay here. I'm going back to check it out. Don't move, Victoria. You understand me? Don't budge an inch. If you see anyone coming, move slowly back into the cover of the trees. If I'm not back in an hour, get back to camp."

Tory watched him until he blended into the shadows at the edge of the village and faded from sight. *Please God, let him come back within the hour.* She had no intention of finding her way back across those rocks alone. She shivered as she remembered those days and nights in that house.

Okay. It had been stupid not to tell him that she'd been held there. She hadn't thought it was important. She just wanted him to find Alex and bring him home. The last thing she'd imagined was that he would haul her all over God's creation and bring her back here.

Besides, those goons had eventually believed her and let her go, so it was no big deal. Was it?

They had done a little more than "hit" her. By the time she arrived in Naples, she was so weak from lack of food and the beatings that she'd collapsed at the airport. She'd been taken to the hospital. There she'd been treated with what she thought was a pretty cavalier attitude. They'd believed that her husband had beaten her, and Victoria didn't tell them any differently.

She rested her head against the olive tree and kept her eyes firmly fixed on the spot where Marc had disappeared. She didn't want to remember what they had done to her. The pain had been excruciating. The terror had been worse. It had surpassed her worst nightmare, because never in her wildest imagination had she conceived of a human being doing what they had done to her.

What had made it a million times worse was that she'd felt Alex close by. Alex had known *exactly* what they were doing to her and had been powerless to stop them. Tears welled in her eyes and she gritted her teeth.

It didn't matter what they did to her. She would do anything to get her brother away from them. Tory pressed the heel of her hand against her eyes, willing the useless tears away.

"Alex, where are you?"

The soft Mediterranean-night wind stole her words away. She squeezed her eyes closed and prayed as she'd never prayed before.

"Did you find anything?" she asked eagerly, dusting the dirt off her backside when Marc came back almost an hour later.

"A canary and a sleeping *signora*. Let's get back to camp."

It was worse going back. Thick clouds had covered the moon, making it impossible for Victoria to see one foot in front of the other. Marc, on the other hand, seemed to have perfect vision as he pushed her up one side of an enormous boulder, then practically dragged her down the next.

They were climbing to the mouth of the grotto when he finally spoke.

"They have him in Pavina."

Victoria let him pull her up another boulder before she asked breathlessly, "How do you know?"

"Don't ask." He let go of her hand and let her follow him around the edge of the sapphire lake, which glowed its calming blue.

He didn't want to tell her he'd bumped into one of her friends on the second floor of that house. And he sure as hell didn't want her to know she would never be bothered by that slimy bastard again. The guy had a hard head. Marc flexed his fingers as he stormed back into the camp.

Marc pulled the Walther from his belt, checking it before he laid it next to the pallet. "We'll go into Pavina tomorrow night." He pulled his black T-shirt over his head.

Victoria couldn't tear her eyes away from sleek muscles and taut brown skin. An arrow of crisp, curling dark hair ran down his washboard-flat stomach to the waistband of his jeans. He started unzipping his fly, and Tory swallowed audibly as a vee of paler skin was exposed. The jeans flew across the sand as he freed his legs—long, hard muscles and hair-roughened tanned skin. Marc, in skimpy black briefs, settled himself comfortably on top of the silver thermal blanket.

"Best get some sleep, princess. Tomorrow is going to be a long day." He pillowed his arms beneath his head, his eyes narrowed as he watched her. Tory picked up his jeans and folded them. She set them down neatly by the water bottle and picked up his shirt. It smelled like him, hot and sexy. She forced herself to fold it neatly on top of the jeans.

"I slept all day. I'm not tired." There was nothing else to tidy. Her grandmother would have said she had ants in her pants. She would have been partially right.

It annoyed her that Marc looked so relaxed while she was as wound up as a watch spring. She wished that he'd left his jeans on. Unwillingly, her eyes traveled down the long length of his practically naked body.

"Come over here, then," he said, his voice silky soft in the half-light. "I'll show you what we can do instead of sleeping."

Tory grabbed the bar of soap out of the pack and picked up a damp towel. "I'm going to take a bath."

Marc closed his eyes, a small smile playing around his mouth. "Don't wake me when you come to bed."

He made it sound so . . . intimate. She scowled as she walked out of camp. As soon as she saw the hot steaming water in the small circular pool she started pulling the damp sweatshirt over her head. The leggings were a one-handed challenge.

Tory slid slowly into the water. Resting the cast on the rim of rock, she closed her eyes as the hot water soothed her aching muscles. Soaping herself quickly, Tory felt her skin jump as her hand skimmed her body. What would it be like...? She pushed *that* thought out of her mind.

Marc Savin was dangerous; he made her think of things she'd never imagined. He made her want things that she'd only read about. How could just spending a few days with the man turn her thoughts from rational to irrational?

Again, the nebulous thought of his hand on her breast made her skin shiver. Oh, God. All she could think about when he was anywhere near her was his touch on her bare skin. Somehow the combination of danger and the proximity of Marc Savin were causing her to have a mental aberration. Yes, that was it. There was something compellingly erotic about the danger mixed with an unhealthy dose of pent-up sexual frustration on her part. Lord only knew what was really on *his* mind.

She would never fit into his life. He *liked* danger. She'd seen the anticipation on his face as they'd skulked around the streets of Pescarna.

She just wanted to find Alex and go back to her quiet, predictable, normal life. She wanted to go back to her color co-ordinated wardrobe—so what if it was all neutrals? She wanted her comfortable eight-to-five job at the auto-parts store.

She *didn't like* adventure. It was fine to read about it, but she was already good and sick of living it. And Marc Savin scared her, most of all. It wasn't just the fact that he held a gun like a natural extension of his arm; when he'd kissed her she'd forgotten every single thing Grandmother had ever warned her about. And there had been a ton of warnings over the years.

Shivering despite the hot water, she laid the tie from the end of her braid carefully on her folded clothes and let her hair fan around her in the water. She wanted shampoo and conditioner—not soap that smelled like Marc Savin. Impatiently she lathered her hair and sank under the hot water to rinse it.

Marc Savin wasn't for her. They were as different as chalk from cheese. When she got back to her real world she would forget all about him and get on with her life. The only reason her mind was filled with him at all was because of his close proximity.

Something brushed her foot and slithered around her ankle. She gave a piercing shriek, shooting up out of the water and scraping her leg on the rocks.

"What the hell is it now?" Marc came up behind her as she stood shivering on the bank. He held a flashlight in one hand and a gun in the other. He played the flashlight on her face.

Tory squinted into the light, her heart pounding. "There's . . . there's something in the water." She shuddered as the water from her clinging wet hair dripped down her bare legs.

He turned the light on the rippling surface of the pond. "Yeah, I can see how this could scare the hell out of you." An annoying little smile played around the corners of his mouth as he trained the narrow beam into the steaming water. A piece of vine, no more than six inches long, swirled in the churned-up sand on the bottom.

Tory gritted her teeth. How was she supposed to have seen it? Mr. Macho had kept the flashlight with him. She glanced down to see that she was standing dripping on her neatly folded clothes. And she was naked—again. With a gargled moan she picked up the soaking clothes and hugged them to her chest. "Turn around," she begged, her face flaming.

Marc turned around. Directing the full force of his pale eyes on her naked skin. Up and down, down and up. She felt the heat of his gaze like a caress. Her heart stopped, then started beating triple time as he flicked off the flashlight, plunging them into shadow.

The faint sapphire glow from the lake illuminated the hard plane of his cheekbones. His eyes glittered dangerously, as he watched her, as if he couldn't help himself.

She could see his body quite clearly in the soft iridescent glow of the water. Which meant he could see her just as clearly—see the trickle of water trembling on the tip of her breast. She clutched the wet clothes tighter to her midriff, until her hand hurt.

With sudden insight, she realized just why they had been dancing around each other ever since they had met. She might not have experienced this intense emotion before, but she recognized it now. It was, God help her, an erotic attraction that had slowly, relentlessly built to this moment.

Tory felt another tickle of water beading on her breast, and saw his eyes follow its path. Mesmerized, she stood absolutely still, feeling her blood heat and surge through her body.

His muscles flexed under satin-smooth skin. "Princess," he warned in a strange deep tone that made her nerve endings shiver. "Now would be a great time to cut and run."

He stepped closer, his footsteps muffled on the springy turf surrounding the pool. He was so close she could feel the heat and power of his hard body all the way down her naked torso. His hand came up to push her wet hair back over one shoulder. His touch was gentle, but his voice was harsh.

"Run."

"I . . . can't." If her life depended on it, Tory couldn't have moved right then.

He sighed. "Drop the clothes, Victoria."

The bundle of damp clothing fell to rest near her bare feet. She tilted her face up to look at him.

His finger traced over her mouth. "That damn stubborn chin of yours . . ."

He drew in a sharp breath as he moved the rest of her long hair over the other shoulder until she stood exposed before him. His shadowy eyes swept over her body. She stopped breathing for a moment, feeling strangely euphoric as she saw the rapid rise and fall of his chest just inches away from her breasts.

Involuntarily her own fingers reached out to touch the springy mat of hair on his chest. His fingers slipped down her bare arm to hold her hand in place. "Do you know what you're doing?"

She felt the wild tattoo of his heartbeat under her palm, and curled her fingers against the muscle and hot skin. An electric sensation shivered up her arm. Her wet hair clung to her back as she swayed closer.

"I'm hoping that you know enough for both of us."

His mouth found hers, and Tory closed her eyes as she felt him part her lips with the delicious heat of his tongue. A low thrill surged through her body as he kissed her until she was light-headed, his mouth moist and insistent as he urged her to respond.

Tory forgot how to breathe as he dragged his mouth away from hers, then claimed her lips again in a series of deep kisses that had her straining on tip-toe against the wall of his chest. She couldn't seem to get close enough.

When he finally lifted his mouth, she gulped drafts of air into her starved lungs.

Taking a handful of her wet hair, he drew it with maddening slowness across her breasts. "If you had any idea..." His voice was thick as he smoothed the strands down her breasts, across the quivering curve of her belly and down. Her hair was cool against her naked skin but she could feel the heat of Marc's fingers. Her skin felt ultrasensitive as his incredibly inventive hands trailed to the very ends of her hair.

His callused fingers dipped fleetingly into the crease between her thighs. Tory thought she might fly out of her skin.

"If you knew what fantasies I've had about your hair..." he whispered.

His hand slid up her narrow rib-cage and covered her damp breast. Her nipple was so engorged that it actually hurt, demanding attention. Her body swayed toward him as he smoothed both hands across the aching peaks. Her head felt unbearably heavy and she dropped it to his chest. When she opened her mouth against his throat, his hot skin tasted slightly salty, and she could feel the thundering of his heartbeat.

"Victoria," he said hoarsely, warningly. She kissed his throat again, passionately. He pressed the hard ridge of his arousal against her thigh to caution her.

"Make love to me," she whispered against his skin. "Please, Marc, make love to me." Her cool hands skimmed the small of his back as she tried to pull him even closer.

"Victoria . . . Tory . . ." He wanted to argue that this was neither the time nor the place. That she was as far from his type of woman as it was possible to get. It defied logic, that she would feel so incredibly perfect against him, that her breast fit his hand perfectly, that her satin skin seemed made for his touch.

He gritted his teeth as her hand skimmed across his stomach. "I hope to hell one of us knows what we're doing," Marc muttered, his voice ragged.

Tory felt the muscles under her hand tighten as he hesitated. She felt powerful. Invincible. Gloriously unafraid. She slid her hand down to the waistband of his briefs.

He clutched her wrist and held it away, his mouth coming down on hers in another bruising kiss. Tory released her arm, clinging to his sleek muscled back. His body was hard and heavy as he lowered her onto the cool bed of moss.

His mouth, fixed on hers, was greedy, devouring. He seemed to want to absorb her. He kissed her hotly, insistently, and she gave back to him, tasting, savoring the dark flavor of him.

He lowered his mouth to taste one breast and Tory jerked as his hair brushed her skin. The touch of his hot, wet mouth on her breast was electrifying.

She felt the rasp of his teeth on her nipple, and she arched her back as the hard length of his arousal pressed at the juncture of her thighs. Moaning, she greedily ran her mouth over any part of him she could reach. He tasted so good, she couldn't get enough of him. His skin was like hot satin here, rough there. She savored every new texture.

With his hands, followed by his open mouth, he caressed every exposed part of her—first her thighs, then down the length of her legs until she moved restlessly against him.

Tory's eyes fluttered open as he rose to strip off his underwear. Her heart jolted as she saw how aroused he was. She had done that.

He knelt down between her legs, his eyes dark, his chest moving rapidly as he sucked in much-needed air. With hands that were steady, he draped her hair with teasingly slow precision until it covered her from crown to thighs.

When it was done to his satisfaction he parted the strands so that her breasts, pale in the magic glow of the water, rose like two pink islands in a sea of dark hair. Victoria shivered from the heat of his gaze as he slowly moved his hands to the juncture of her thighs, his concentration frustrating and complete. She wanted him to hurry, but he moved with methodical precision to untangle her long tresses from the nest of short curls at the apex of her thighs. Then, gripping both her arms, he settled them above her head so that she lay suppliant and exposed before him.

"Perfect." The heat of his pale eyes was like a physical caress as he scrutinized her. But she wanted more. The blanket of wet hair stuck to her skin, tickling nerves already screaming for his touch.

She licked her lips, groaning when he cupped both breasts in his hands. Her aching nipples were soothed momentarily as he took each hard bud between his fingers, rotating them. An instant later, he settled his hot, wet mouth on one peak, drawing it in, teasing excruciatingly with his tongue. When his hand trailed down, over the swell of her hip and tangled in the curls at the juncture of her thighs, she gasped.

He opened her with his fingers, and she felt his first intimate touch. Her body arched reflexively. She cried out as two fingers slipped inside her. Her vision blurred, and she clutched a handful of the sweet-smelling grass above her head.

"Marc . . ." she whispered beseechingly.

He stared into her eyes, the tendons in his neck rigid as he groaned through clenched teeth. "God, you're wonderfully responsive." Again his fingers moved inside her, creating a tension that had her moving restlessly, hungrily, against his hand.

She bit her lip as he lowered his face to the cradle of her thighs. Her fingers tangled in his hair. It felt silky smooth as it skimmed his broad tanned shoulders. A wash of intense emotion gripped her—she wanted to absorb him totally. Parting her lips, she drew in a ragged breath.

Tory struggled to draw air into her starved lungs as he rocked his hips against hers. Her body felt swollen and ready to burst as he kept up the steady rhythm.

"Please..." She tightened her fingers in his hair. "Oh, please. I . . . need you . . . inside."

He ground the rock-hard ridge of his arousal against her pelvic bone again and again. "You're not ready."

4

NOT READY? Feelings she had no control over shimmered through her body. Her cry, as she climaxed, ricocheted against the cave walls and echoed deep inside her.

Dimly she heard Marc rasp, "Now you're ready!" and he entered her. The pain was brief, her need greater. Tory wrapped her legs around his waist, thinking she would die of pleasure. She rose and fell with him as he moved in and out in a maddening rhythm that had her moaning his name.

Her mouth open, wild for his kisses, Tory dug her nails into his back. His hands came down to cup her bottom, lifting her so he could thrust more deeply inside her. Tory caught the edge of the wave, her hips countering his until he stiffened, and with a final thrust, carried them both over the top of a tidal wave.

Tory wrapped her arm around his sweat-drenched back and felt the muscles tense as she held him. She welcomed the heavy weight sprawled on top of her as she struggled to regulate her breathing. She could hear water dripping somewhere in the cave. Marc's breath tickled the side of her neck, cooling her hot skin.

A lump formed in her throat as she caressed his skin, finding first one ridge of scars, then another. She tried to soothe those long-ago hurts. Her eyelids were heavy, she was emotionally drained as his weight pressed her into the soft sand.

Just before she slid unwillingly into sleep, she heard him swear.

MARC WAS LIVID. At himself and at her. What a dammed foolish thing to do. He pulled away from her limp body and stood, looking down at her, sprawled seductively against the sand and emerald ground cover.

He scrubbed his eyes and then dropped his hand when he smelled her there. "Damn."

Tossing the other blanket over her tempting body, he pulled a flask out of his pack and took a fortifying swig. The whiskey burned his tongue, then made a satisfyingly cleansing trail down his throat.

He reluctantly capped the flask and stuck it deep in the pocket of the pack. No point in compounding the problem.

She'd lied. Those weeks she'd spent courtesy of Spider had been no cakewalk. He'd managed to squeeze enough information out of the guy back at the pink house to make bile rise in his throat.

She was a civilian, damn it! Marc rose and dressed, keeping his gaze firmly averted from the sleeping woman. He was dying for a cigarette and he didn't even smoke.

What in the hell was going on here? His training made it possible for him to clear his mind of the sexual fog, although to his annoyance it wasn't that easy.

T-FLAC had been after the terrorist group called Spider for more than seven years. Only after Lynx had gone in under cover more than a year ago had they discovered that *two* men ran the organization—Samuel Hoag and Christoph Ragno.

They knew of Ragno. He'd been a drug dealer in South America when he'd disappeared for about two years. Phantom had never run into him while he was under cover, but he'd heard plenty about Ragno's ruthlessness.

Hoag had appeared out of nowhere. No one knew anything about him. At this point it was immaterial. The Spider group was into any illegal activity that offered a quick profit. From Prague to Pretoria the group was small and absolutely invisible. And so far, invincible.

Marc paced the small area while his mind raced. That they had let Victoria go didn't make any damned sense. Just as he wanted to stop Spider, Spider wanted to stop him—or rather, Savage.

Once they connected Lynx to Phantom, they had set the trap. Made sure that the mutilated body had been found by the right people.

It was an explanation, but it wasn't that feasible. There were only three people who knew who Savage was. Himself, Lynx, and now Victoria Jones.

He'd recruited Lynx himself. He'd trained him, and Marc knew without a doubt that nothing, up to and including death, would make his agent turn.

Victoria Jones, on the other hand, had been on the island for two weeks. She was bright enough to take what her brother had told her in his letter and embellish it until she came up with something damn close to the truth. It wouldn't have taken much for Spider's henchmen to break her.

Whether she'd meant to or not, there was a good possibility that Victoria had given Spider exactly what they wanted—Phantom.

Leaving Victoria, Marc picked up the Uzi and headed outside.

Resting the weapon on his drawn-up leg, he gazed out across the open expanse of rain-tossed ocean. Heavy rain poured from a charcoal-gray sky. The air smelled fresh and clean.

He couldn't remember the last time he'd thought with his balls. He ground his teeth and fingered the trigger of the Uzi. He wanted to let go and spray the rain with bullets. He wanted someone to come around that corner so that he could pound his fist into their bones and feel their flesh split.

Rain pounded from a dark sky. Sea-spray painted the rocks and boulders below him. The scent of Victoria Jones had seeped into the membrane of his nostrils, blocking out the smell of ozone and salt. Blocking out common sense. This was not good, not good at all. He had to make sure this didn't happen again. She was going to get him killed if he didn't start thinking with a more rational part of his anatomy.

God help him, he still didn't trust her. Just how far would she go to save her brother? Stupid question. She'd do anything, betray anyone, to ensure Lynx's safety. Just for a moment there, when he'd looked down into those clear green eyes, just before he'd buried himself in the warmth of her body, he'd felt a flickering of hope. Which just went to show what an idiot he was.

What he had to do was make her go back to being afraid of him. They would both be safer that way.

"What are you doing out here?"

Her voice came from directly behind him and he sprang to his feet, the Uzi pressed to her heart.

She was wearing one of his black T-shirts that hit her midthigh and left the mouth-watering length of her pale slender legs bare. He knew damn well she was naked underneath. Her small plump breasts molded the thin cotton. He steeled himself. This was do-or-die time. He pressed the ugly mouth of the gun between her breasts.

Tory's eyes widened. The delectable, pale pink lips curved into a tentative smile. "I'm sorry," she whispered huskily. "I didn't mean to scare you."

Marc hardened his heart and forced the rest of his body to relax. "You scare me, all right, honey, but not in the way you think." He lowered the Uzi. He turned away to look out at the churning ocean.

He felt her tentative touch on his bare arm and shrugged it away. "Go back to camp."

"Are you coming to bed soon?"

"Thanks, but no thanks." His voice was flat. "I've had my sex for tonight." Marc hitched his bare foot on the rock behind him and rested the gun on his knee.

"Why...why...?" She swallowed audibly as she tried to find the words.

"Spit it out, honey." A wave shot thirty feet in the air in a burst of white spume. "Why what?"

"Why are you talking to me like this?"

Marc turned to look at her. There was a crease of confusion between her brows and she was biting her lower lip. *Make it good, pal.* "You think because I took your virginity I should give you a promise and a ring? Get a life, lady. Sex is sex."

Her hand flashed out with surprising speed, connecting with his cheek a split second before he caught her wrist in a punishing hold.

His face stung. Under his fingers he felt the small delicate bones of her wrist. "I warned you before: Don't ever hit unless you expect to be hit back," Marc said tightly, giving her wrist a warning squeeze. "You seem to be under the mistaken belief that I'm a gentleman. I'm not."

"Would you please let go," she said with frigid politeness. "You're hurting me." He let go, watching her, keeping his eyes cold, as she rubbed at the red marks with fingers that shook.

"No one," Tory countered, "would ever mistake you for anything other than what you are." Her cheeks flamed with obvious fury. "You're hard and cruel and a...a bully! Why don't you go ahead and hit me back? Maybe it would make you feel more like a man!"

"Don't tempt me," he said tightly, leaning against the rock, the marks of her fingers a burning brand on his face.

"You're despicable." He saw the way her hand trembled as she suddenly realized that he was bare-ass naked. Her eyes shot from his erection to his face and stayed there, her cheeks scarlet.

"Despicable? Lady, you ain't seen nothing yet." He laughed unpleasantly, enjoying the way her eyes flashed, the way those soft pink lips tightened. He rubbed at the puckered scar on his shoulder—just to remind himself.

Then she made the fatal mistake of tilting her chin at him.

With a smoothness that belied his jerking pulse, he pulled her hard against him. "You liked it." He looked down at her tense face. "Is that it, baby? You want more good old sex." He trailed his hand down the damp satin of her hair, pulling her hips into the cradle of his own with a jerk that caught her off balance.

He kissed her hard, roughly forcing her mouth open and thrusting his tongue into the remembered sweetness. She tried to close her mouth and he used his free hand to squeeze her jaw. The other hand pressed her more tightly against his arousal.

"Like that? Is this what you want, green eyes? Do you like it rough? Does it turn you on to know that just looking at you makes me hard?"

She struggled in his arms. "Let . . . me . . . go!"

He let her go with a suddenness that surprised them both. She rubbed her arm over her swollen mouth and glared at him. "Don't ever come near me again." Her voice was rock steady as she dropped her arm.

Marc picked up the gun he'd dropped and pulled out the clip to check for sand. He looked at her over his shoulder. "Was it worth losing your virginity to save your precious brother?" The metallic clink as he snapped the clip back couldn't smother the sound of her gasp.

"It wasn't like that," she said furiously, stepping toward him.

Anger and resentment flared through him—how easily she got under his skin and past his defenses. "I'll give you ten seconds to get your treacherous butt back to camp." He said it coldly, his gaze running the length of her legs, then lifting to focus on the rapid rise and fall of her breasts.

"All I want to know—"

"Three."

"—is why you're—"

"Four."

"Please! Just stop count—"

"Five."

"Stop doing that! Please, just tell me what I—"

"Seven. Eight. Nine. Go!" Marc cocked the gun and pointed it at her heart. She wasn't afraid of the dammed gun, but her eyes widened as she saw what was in his eyes.

She ran.

THE CAMP WAS as they'd left it. With jerky movements she folded the blankets, stuffing them behind the pack against the wall. Her jaw was clenched in absolute fury.

Fury was an infinitely better emotion than humiliation. Dressing quickly just in case he should come back, she made herself a cup of coffee and sat against the wall.

She should have known better. She did know better. Except that it had seemed so inevitably right. On the other hand, she thought grimly, Marc Savin brought out a host of untoward emotions that she'd never experienced before, most of which she didn't like.

It wasn't like her to lose her temper. Yet she'd lost it more times than she could count with Marc Savin. She was deeply ashamed of how satisfying it had been to slap him. Twice.

It wasn't in her to argue back, either, but she'd found that once she started, it was actually a very energizing experience.

This whole experience was disconcerting. Worst of all was feeling the way she didn't want to feel about the man who was going to find her brother. She didn't want to love Marc Savin, but love him she did. It might not be rational but there she was. She bit down on her bottom lip.

Their differences were insurmountable. She would go back to San Diego when this was all over and get on with her beige life. He would forget her as soon as she was out of sight. This was a moment out of time, a sliver of excitement in her otherwise predictable existence. When this adventure was over, she knew she would never see Marc Savin again—if she happened to survive it.

Later, she would take out these moments with Marc and hold them to the light. She wished she understood him. She was absolutely baffled by his anger. He had her confused half the time and wanting to get closer the rest of the time. The best thing she could do was roll with the punches. If he wanted to act as if their lovemaking was no big deal, then so be it.

Brushing the sand off her leggings, Tory reluctantly stood. Marc Savin could stay away all day, for all she cared. *She* was hungry.

Setting up the little stove, she randomly picked up one of the foil food pouches. It made absolutely no difference which one she chose, they all seemed to taste the same. Pretty much anything would have to taste better than the "eggs" Marc had served her yesterday.

The food tasted terrible but it filled the hole in her stomach and killed about five minutes. Next she emptied the A.L.I.C.E. pack and cataloged the contents. It appeared he was ready for anything. There were several guns, which she gingerly set aside, knives that looked lethal, what looked like a slingshot, and more C-rations or M.R.E.'s. There was a shovel and miscellaneous other items for which she didn't even want to know the uses.

Tory refolded and tightly rolled half-a-dozen black T-shirts and pairs of socks, then shoved them in the bottom. Putting aside the compass and several maps of Marezzo to go on top, she neatly repacked the backpack so that she knew where everything was.

Tory then took the bar of soap, gathered all their soiled clothes and carried everything to the pool. Grateful to have something to do that would take her mind off Marc, she set about washing, rinsing and squeezing. It was fairly warm in the cave, so if she washed and wrung things out really well, they should be dry within a few hours. She laid the damp clothing out beside the pool and returned to camp.

Glancing around, she sighed in frustration. Everything was neat and tidy and in its place. Even the "bed" was straightened out. She wished she knew what time it was. On the way back from the lake she'd ambled to the entrance, where she'd seen the last rays of the sun as it dipped to the horizon.

Marc still wasn't back. Where could he have gone? She refused to worry. Lying down, she curled on her side, facing the entrance so that she would see him returning.

SHE HEARD THE SOFT whisper of sand under his bare feet, and squeezed her eyes shut. Marc stood over her, his legs spread.

"Go away."

He tossed the gun in the general vicinity of the pack, where it landed with a soft thud. "My bed, my blanket."

Victoria scrambled to her feet, her eyes wary. She wasn't going to give an inch. "Fine. You can have it." She stormed across and yanked at the other blanket, the Uzi dropping nose first into the sand. "It's cool in here. I need both blankets," he said.

"Put on some clothes, then." Her voice was thick with tears and filled with anger. "I'll sleep over here." She fanned the silver-foil blanket and settled it on the ground as far away from him as she could.

It took Marc three seconds to flip her off it onto the sand. He looked down at her sprawled body. The T-shirt rode to her waist. She was in full armor, bra and all. She was also absolutely livid. Which was exactly what he wanted. Wasn't it?

She got up and remade their bed. Marc was determined to be obstinate, but she wasn't going to let him see how much he annoyed her. She lay down on the bed and closed her eyes. She knew he was watching her. "Don't even think about touching me." She began to count.

She'd reached two thousand and seven when she felt Marc settle down next to her. He didn't touch her.

SHE AWOKE TO FIND her back snuggled into the curve of his body. Two things became immediately apparent. One was the hard ridge of his arousal pressing insistently at her bottom. The other was Marc's fingers tenderly, and with devastating effect, manipulating her already aroused nipple.

Tory groaned softly as the pressure increased from behind and his hand trailed down her rib cage and lower until it slid beneath the skintight leggings and came to the nest of curls at the juncture of her thighs.

She could feel the moisture as her body readied itself for his lovemaking, and she clamped her legs tightly together, trapping his wandering hand between them. She gritted her teeth as his other arm slid under her and his fingers cupped her breast.

He was fast asleep. Tory forced herself to lie still. Why couldn't he *talk* in his sleep like a normal person? In a moment he would stop. Wouldn't he?

For a moment the movement of his hands did stop, and she let out the shaky breath she'd been holding.

When he spoke into her ear, she almost jumped out of her skin.

"Open your legs to me, green eyes."

Tory clenched the muscles in her thighs as she felt his fingers move against her. "Stop that. . . ." He cleverly slipped one long finger into the slick folds as he pressed her hard against him.

With barely exerted pressure he turned her onto her back. Tory looked up at his face looming above her. The hard line of his jaw was blurred under the dark, bristly shadow of several days' growth of beard. His pale eyes glittered.

Tory pushed his hair out of his eyes as he leaned over her. "This isn't fair," she said weakly, her arm circling his neck as his head blocked out the soft sapphire glow from the lake.

His lips touched hers—softly, gently. Tory found her fingers tightening in the thick hair at his nape; as if in response, his lips moved more insistently on hers and his tongue invaded her mouth. She closed her eyes as sensation washed over her. Her T-shirt was up around her throat, her bra loose and hanging, as her soft breasts were pressed flat against the hard wall of his chest.

She felt the pounding of his heart syncopating in perfect rhythm with her own. Her skin felt alive as he drew his hand under her head and swept her hair out of the way. It would be full of sand, but she didn't care.

"You're pure hell on my good intentions—you know that, princess?" Marc lifted his head to look down at her. "I can't believe that you're still here," he said roughly, his mouth tilting in a wry smile.

She lifted her arms as he stripped her. "Where else would I be?"

"As far the hell away from me as you could get."

"We're on an island. How far could I go?" she countered softly, her eyes far too forgiving.

Marc squeezed his eyes shut for a moment. "Hell, Victoria, you don't have a self-preserving bone in your body, do you?"

Obviously the ploy he'd used had backfired. So much for that idea. He used his thumb to rub her bottom lip, his eyes locked with hers. The tip of Victoria's tongue came out and Marc was lost. She took a little nip from his thumb and he retaliated by crushing her to him, devouring her mouth until she was weak.

He kissed her with an intensity and dedication that would have awed her if she'd been in her right mind. When he eventually broke the kiss they were both breathing hard. Then his clever lips moved down her throat and she felt the wet heat of his open mouth on her nipple. She kneaded the damp skin of his back as he lavished his attention first on one hard peak and then the other. Tory realized that she was making small insistent noises in the back of her throat.

He wouldn't be hurried, though. With slow thoroughness his mouth moved down her rib cage. Her skin was on fire as his fingers opened her, and as predictably as a sunrise his mouth found her. She couldn't help herself; her legs moved restlessly under the onslaught as his lips and tongue brought her right to the edge.

She wanted him. Now. "Marc . . . please, oh, please . . ." She clutched at his hair until he moved back up her body and settled into the cradle of her thighs. He surged into her and her climax came forcefully and immediately.

He held her in the harbor of his strong arms until the shudders that racked her body died away. And then he started to move again as if he'd never stopped.

Victoria's head thrashed in the sand. "No...more... I can't...."

But she realized with amazement that she could, when she felt his powerful hands grip her bottom and his steady thrust become harder, faster, deeper.

"Come with me, Victoria. Come with me." His voice was harsh in her ear, as he drove into her again and again.

"Yes . . . Like that . . ." He inhaled sharply as her hips rose, then she felt his hands slide under her as he clutched her bottom, showing her how to move. "God! Yes . . . yes . . . !"

Astounded she felt her muscles gather and tense, and when he gave one last surge, his shout was echoed by hers.

Her body tightened and soared, then dissolved in a heap beneath him as he collapsed against her, his breath ragged against her throat.

Her hair had been tossed about and Marc moved a strand from where it stuck to her hot, damp cheek. "God, you're so beautifully responsive," he murmured. His hand lingered on her face as he looked down at her with a slightly bemused expression. "When I look at you, all I can think about are clean sheets on a big bed."

"We seem to have done all right on the ground," Tory said shyly, smoothing the frown between his eyes with one finger.

He took her hand from his face and kissed her fingertips before rolling onto his back, taking her with him. Her chin rested on his chest where his heart still beat an excited tattoo under her breast.

Sliding down so his chest pillowed her cheek, Tory smoothed her hand down the hard flat muscles, her fingers playing with the crisp dark hairs. She felt his lips on her hair.

"Talk to me," he said.

Perfectly relaxed and content in the semidarkness, Tory complied. She told him how, when she'd been a young child, her grandmother had been a night nurse, and the house had always been closed up and dark during the day so that the woman could sleep. She told him of her heartache over her grandmother's refusal to adopt Alex or allow him to visit his sister.

Tory said little about her bookkeeping job and skirted around his question about whom she'd dated. Her grandmother had refused to allow her the usual freedoms granted most teenagers and by the time she had died and Tory was living on her own, she'd felt painfully out of her depth with the men she met.

Victoria nuzzled closer to Marc, blissfully happy. "Have you ever been in love?" As soon as the words left her mouth she regretted saying them. Even if she had no experience, she knew better than to expect a declaration of love from a man like Marc Savin.

"Don't be getting any ideas here, green eyes. I'm not a stick-around kind of guy. You know that."

There was a lump the size of a fist in her throat. "Why not?" Her voice was thick. She'd gone this far—

"Too many people I cared about have—" *Betrayed me*, he thought, and replaced it with, "Been taken away from me, Victoria. I just don't trust the hell out of fate."

"What if I trust it enough for both of us?"

There was a long pause. "I'm incapable of loving anyone, Victoria. I've seen too much to ever have the naive belief that love will conquer all. Any excess emotion makes a man weak, be it love or hate. I can't afford to be off guard. My life and those of my operatives depend on my having a clear head."

"And an empty heart."

He tilted her chin up so that her eyes met his. "I want you more than I've ever wanted another woman—if that means anything."

"Does it to you?" she asked wistfully, and felt his other hand cup her bottom to draw her upward.

"Yes." His mouth was less than a whisper away as he breathed the words like a prayer: "Yes, God help me. It's all I've got to give."

"Who hurt you, Marc? What woman made you lose the ability to love?"

"What makes you think that there ever *was* a woman?"

Tory regarded him steadily. "Because I know that someone hurt you very badly. Because sometimes when you look at me, and I can see how much you want me, you rub at this scar on your shoulder and then the heat goes out of your eyes and you try to make me hate you."

Marc eased her down so that her face was pressed against the mat of hair on his chest. Tory felt his lungs expand as he took a deep breath. She wanted to see his face while he was talking, but she stayed where she was, with his heart beating under her cheek.

"Her name was Krista Davis...."

"Blue eyes, silky blond hair," Tory guessed. "A chest out to there. A petite Barbie doll who could probably shoot a gun beside you all day and then be home in time to cook a gourmet dinner. Probably wearing a black negligee. Every man's fantasy—lucky you."

"Ever heard the expression, 'Be careful what you wish for'?"

"Oh, yes. My grandmother said it all the time. I learned early to keep my 'wishes' few and far between. And small." When Marc's arms tightened around her she prodded him with her chin. "Go on."

"Mmm. I recruited and trained Krista myself. She was one of my best operatives. God, she was quick as lightning. Krista would size up a situation and handle it before any of my other people had even realized that there might be a problem. She was absolutely fearless. Afraid of nothing."

Bully for her! Courage and cleavage! "I don't need to know the details," she said tightly. "Just hit the main points."

"Jealous?"

"Yes. Just finish."

"We worked together on several jobs. She was an excellent shot, I trusted her with my life. We had been lovers for a year before we planned on getting married. Krista's idea, but hell, I liked the idea of a wife. Having someone to come home to. Kids . . ." He was silent for a moment and Tory sensed that whatever he was about to say would be terrible.

"I . . . I'd gone under cover in Mexico City. Drugs. The big guys. I'd been under cover for seven months. Everything was copacetic until Krista arrived on the scene.

"'Backup,' she said. She played her damn part too well. I believed her. She betrayed me. The mission was scrubbed. More fool me."

"Not all women are like that," Tory murmured. She laid her cheek against his, then pressed closer, wanting to absorb his pain. Tears stung her eyes.

"Krista isn't like that anymore, either. She's dead. But I'll never let anyone else that close again." His voice was cold. "I value my own hide too much to take the chance."

"Did you love Krista?"

"No. But it was as close as I can get. I told you not to get ideas. Sex is all I can offer you. Take it or leave it."

She met his gaze with a clear-eyed look that went to his heart like a laser. "I'll take it."

He rolled her onto her back, sliding his hands up her arms until he wove his fingers through hers, palm to palm, heart to heart. He knew that he was heavy, but she lay perfectly relaxed beneath him, looking up at him.

"You'll take it?"

"Yes."

For a moment Marc rested his forehead against hers. "What did I do to deserve you?"

"You must have been a very good boy at sometime in your misspent youth." Her mouth found his and she gave him a too-brief kiss that left him wanting more. She looked up at him, her eyes sparkling. "I'm hungry."

"Yeah?" He gave her a lecherous look and she pushed at his shoulder.

"For food."

"Too bad."

"You can say that again. Those packaged things are awful."

Rolling off her, he got to his feet and held out his hand. "Up and at 'em, green eyes. Let's go for a swim before we eat." Swooping down, he pressed a still-hungry kiss to her swollen lips.

BACK AT CAMP, Marc heated four packs of the dreaded "stew" while Victoria dressed. He braided her wet hair tightly, tucking it down inside the back of her T-shirt as he'd done the last time.

"Make sure no one gets a look at this hair. It's too damned memorable." He found a baseball cap stuffed in a side pocket of his pack and pulled it down low over her eyes. "That should do it." Handing her the tin plate, he settled on the sand and began eating.

"It's going to be full light by the time we get into Pavina." He glanced up at her and asked quietly, "Did you go into the town the last time you were here?"

Tory swallowed with difficulty. Marc must have tossed four different meals together. "Yes, I spent a couple of hours there. Then I headed straight for Pescarna because I had such a strong feeling that was where they were holding Alex." She pushed the bill of the cap out of her eyes. "It must be ten miles if not more to Pavina. Surely we're not going to walk?"

"If you weren't with me I would." Marc glanced at her still-full plate. "Are you going to eat that?"

Victoria handed the plate to him more than willingly.

Marc set both empty plates aside when he was done and went to the back of the cave. Crouching down, he opened the A.L.I.C.E. pack. "What the hell were you doing messing around in this pack? Damn it woman, I can't find anything!"

"Everything is where it's supposed to be. I had to find the first-aid kit."

"It was right on top." He started pulling things willy-nilly out of the pack and tossing them on the sand. "Don't start nesting, for God's sake!"

"I tidied it," she said, striving for lightness. She could see that he was spoiling for a fight—again.

"Leave my things the hell alone."

"Would you listen to yourself. Why are you suddenly so angry?"

"I don't like people messing with my gear. I know where everything is and I—"

"Fine." Victoria picked up the plates and got to her feet. "Why don't I just let you rant and rave in private while I go and wash these."

5

WHEN SHE GOT BACK with the clean plates, he was tucking his pant legs into the tops of his boots. His hair had been tied back and he had a gun in his hand.

"What?" Victoria glared at him. "Are you going to shoot me now?"

Marc closed his eyes briefly, then lifted his shirt to tuck the Walther into his waistband at the small of his back. His pale eyes assessed her and his mouth tightened. "You can't go out with that damned cast showing. People will see you a mile away and they'll remember you."

"I'll wear the sweatshirt." Victoria waited until he moved aside and then packed away the clean plates.

"The sweatshirt is soaking wet," Marc said with disgust. "Thanks to your Harriet Homemaker move, washing everything in sight. Jesus, woman, this isn't a little family camping trip, you know!"

"I'll wear the blasted thing wet, okay? I wish you'd be a little more consistent," she muttered crossly. "One minute you're making love to me and the next you've got your knickers in a knot about something or other."

"Knickers in a knot?" Marc suddenly grinned, his foul mood evaporating. "I certainly have something in a knot when I'm around you."

"You know what I mean!"

He looked very tall and menacing as he strode across the sand toward her. She moved her feet slightly apart and tilted her chin. She was getting sick and tired of him sniping and snarling at her.

He had something in his hand, but she couldn't see what it was. Tory held her ground as he came right up to her. He looked like a desperado with his earring flashing and dark stubble shadowing his face.

The smile was gone as he said briskly, "Lift your arms."

If he thought for one second that she was going to kiss him, he had another thing coming. "Why should I?" she asked belligerently, then recoiled when she saw what he was holding. The blood seemed to drain from her head.

"I hope for your sake that you don't plan on using that belt on me!" She saw a flash of another man, strap raised.... Her muscles tensed.

Marc gave her one of his wicked smiles, and she forgot everything in the heat of his pewter gaze. "Have you ever been tied up and had someone make love to you, Victoria?" The loop of the belt came up and stroked her cheek.

She shivered as the smooth leather skimmed down her bare throat. "N-no," she whispered, her voice shaking. "You—you know I haven't." The hard leather belt brushed her nipple through her T-shirt and Tory almost bit off her tongue.

Her eyes locked with his as he caressed her with the belt. She couldn't tell from his expression whether he intended to make love to her again, or if he was just using this as another means to taunt her.

"S-stop that!" She stepped back, away from the unfamiliar and highly erotic feel of the leather.

Marc's hand stilled as he shook his head slightly. "Put on the damned belt, Victoria, and keep the hell away from me."

Tory snatched it out of his hand and tugged it around her waist, cinching it tightly. He brushed her hands aside and tugged the shirt out to cover it. That done to his satisfaction, he grabbed another black shirt and started ripping it to shreds.

He then wrapped her cast in the fabric. "That should do it. I wish I could cut the frigging thing off."

"What? My arm?" She matched his sarcasm, pulling the bill of her cap lower to hide her face.

"That cast is a liability." Marc finished repacking and dragged the pack into the shadows against the back wall, then stripped everything from the shelf and shoved that into the shadows, too. He looked around to make sure everything was well hidden.

"If I recall correctly, I didn't want to come."

"I thought I needed you to find your brother," Marc said disgustedly, cramming a lethal-looking knife into the back of his jeans and blousing his shirt to cover it. He glanced around to see if he'd missed anything.

"You still do," Victoria said tightly. The belt scratched her bare skin. "I don't need a belt with leggings, you know."

"Oh, right. So far you've been such a big help." Marc batted her hand away from her waist. "You need *this* belt. It might save your life."

Tory sighed. "Are you going to let me in on this little 'agent' secret or am I going to have to improvise when something happens? What does this belt do, anyway? Make me into a kung fu expert?"

"I'll keep you informed on a need-to-know basis."

"I need to know now!"

Marc filled a flask from the collapsible water bottle and clipped it to his belt. "Ready?"

"Let's just go. The sooner we find Alex, the sooner I can get back to my life." She followed him out of camp, speaking to his back. "You know what real life is, don't you? That's where people have what's called conversation. That's where civilized people stay in one mood for more than half an hour. That's where people don't go around with who-knows-what wrapped around their waists." She impatiently pushed a fern frond out of her way. "There'd better not be a bomb or anything like that in this stupid belt."

Marc kept walking, moving quickly ahead of her toward the entrance of the cave. "Scared I'll blow you to kingdom come, princess?"

"Nothing you could do would surprise me anymore." She blinked as they emerged from the opening, drawing in deep lungfuls of salty fresh air.

The sky was tinted a pale lavender, the sun just peeking over the horizon in a faint apricot streak. The ocean lay calm and flat like a giant piece of Venetian glass, gilded by the rising sun.

Tory accepted his help down the rocks to the damp sand below. This time, instead of turning right toward Pescarna they headed left, keeping close to the base of the towering limestone cliff.

The few bites of "breakfast" formed a tight knot in Tory's stomach as she hurried to catch up with him. By the time they reached Pavina it would probably be midmorning. There would be people all over the place. Tory shivered. Marc had been right. If just one person recognized her from before, their cover would be blown. Nervously she tugged the T-shirt down in back, feeling the reassuring weight of her braid against her bare skin.

Marc turned to watch her scramble over the rocks buried in the sand. "Get a move on. I want to get there in time to blend in with the crowds at the market."

He slowed his stride enough so that Tory only had to trot to keep up with him. The cast on her arm weighed a ton and became heavier with every step.

"Are you going to make it?"

Her arm hurt and she'd had enough. There was no way she could walk one more step on wet sand, where each step weighed ten tons. He was standing waiting for her reply. Tory tilted her chin. "Of course, I'm going to make it. Lead on."

By the time they reached the end of the high cliff she was panting, and her shirt stuck uncomfortably to her back. Marc moved beneath the shadow of a solitary tree that stood on the low bluff, and unclipped the water bottle from his belt. He uncapped it and handed it to her. "Stay here and rest. I'm going to find some transportation." He vanished over the rise and Tory sank down, hugging her knees to her chest and resting her head on her arms.

She wasn't cut out for this cloak-and-dagger stuff. Marc took this all in his stride. Nice for him. She wanted her brother back. She wanted to return to civilization and a real bed. She wanted real food and a knife and fork. She wanted her nice predictable spreadsheets and ledgers. She wanted to meet a nice, ordinary, *rational* man.

Tory lifted her head and picked up the canvas-covered bottle. The water was lukewarm and tasted slightly of sulfur, but her mouth was parched and she drank greedily before recapping the container and setting it upright in the sand beside her.

The sun was a glorious persimmon ball above the horizon by the time Marc came back. He was wearing a beige linen jacket over his black T-shirt and jeans. The unstructured, creased linen jacket should have looked ridiculous, but instead he looked as though he'd just stepped out of *GQ*. He'd pushed the sleeves up to expose darkly tanned muscular forearms, and there was absolutely no evidence of the arsenal he carried on his body.

"I was in luck. Come on." He pulled her to her feet and attached the bottle to his belt. "I found a farmer who was willing to part with his truck. We'll be in Pavina in about thirty minutes."

He took her hand to pull her up the sandy incline, letting go as soon as they reached flat ground. The truck was parked under a small stand of orange trees. The vehicle looked as if it had survived several wars. It might have been blue, but whatever color it had once been was almost obliterated by rust and enormous dents.

Tory looked at the vehicle dubiously before climbing into the cab, pushing away debris with her feet. The owner had eaten several weeks' worth of breakfasts, lunches and dinners there by the look and smell of the papers and containers on the floor and seat. She wrinkled her nose as Marc got in. He had to slam his door twice before it closed.

The windows didn't open and the smell of garlic and cheap wine was overpowering. The sun beat in on her side of the truck as Marc turned it with a spray of sand and headed down the dirt road.

To the right she could see the high flat peak of Monte Tolaro, an extinct volcano rising thousands of feet into the clear blue sky. Marc turned onto a tarred road and headed west toward Pavina. He relaxed in the vinyl seat, one hand on the wheel, the other resting alongside the window. He glanced at her out of the corner of his eye. Tory kept her face turned toward the vineyards that flashed by.

"What will we do when we find Alex?" She pinched a tomato-encrusted paper between her fingers and tossed it on the floor as she turned more fully to face him.

"When we know exactly where he is, you take the truck back to where I picked you up and go back to the grotto and wait for us. As soon as Lynx and I get back, I'll contact Angelo and we're outta here."

"You make it sound so simple." She gazed intensely at him. "But it won't be. Will it?" Her throat tightened and she had to wait for the threat of tears to pass. "They're holding him somewhere and he's badly hurt."

Marc reached out and linked his fingers with hers on her updrawn knee. "He's trained for just such an eventuality, Victoria. Trust me, I'll get your brother out."

Tory clenched her fingers within the safe harbor of his hand. "Promise?"

Marc squeezed once and then let go to have both hands on the steering wheel as the truck's bald tires fought for purchase on the cobblestones. "Promise."

She believed him. God help her, she did believe he would get Alex out and away safely. The way he treated her was incidental to him saving her brother.

Marc pulled the old pickup in between an open-sided wagon piled high with oranges and a big truck that had a crude bottle of wine painted on the side. He put his hand on her shoulder as she moved to open the door.

"Remember, we are just a couple of tourists interested in market day." He removed the gun and checked it under cover of the cracked dashboard. Pulling the key out of the ignition, he handed it to her.

"I want you to stay as close to me as you can." His eyes scanned her pale face. "You'll do fine. The moment you know where they are holding Alex, just let me know. Walk slowly, look around. And for God's sake," he warned lightly, "don't look so terrified."

"I *am* terrified! What if . . . ?"

He kissed her—just pulled her toward him and locked his arms around her and kissed her hard. It was a kiss totally unlike any of the others. His mouth scorched hers, his arms were like a vise around her and she could feel her heart pounding in her ears. He smelled of clean sweat, and the heady, familiar scent of him made her mouth relax under his.

When he lifted his mouth from hers she wanted to beg him for just one more, but the key dug into the tender flesh of her palm.

He leaned back against the seat and said with satisfaction, "We were being watched. That should do it."

"You...you kissed me like that because someone was watching us?"

Marc adjusted his jacket, checking to make sure his weapons didn't show. "It's called a cover, princess."

"I have nowhere to put the key," she said tightly, so furious she forgot to be scared.

Marc plucked the key out of her hand and hid it under his seat. "This is probably better, anyway. If for some reason we become separated, get your ass back to the truck and get the hell out of here. Got it?"

Victoria nodded and pushed open the door. She squared her shoulders as Marc came around the bed of the truck and took her hand. When this was over she would waste no time in getting as far away from him as she could.

They were jostled by hordes of people moving through the enormous gates of the walled city of Pavina. No vehicular traffic was allowed in and the narrow cobbled streets were crowded with pedestrians. Victoria pressed up against Marc as they allowed the momentum of the crowd to push them toward the piazza, where the weekly market was in full swing.

The scent of oranges, garlic, hot sweaty bodies and wine filled the air. The day had become blisteringly hot and the press of people claustrophobic as they entered the large square.

Vendors had set up their wares in stalls that displayed the brilliant colors of the Mediterranean. The sunshine bright yellow of lemons, the translucent green of the grapes and the glossy black of olives. Some of the stalls were piled high with fruits and vegetables, others groaned under the weight of fresh fish. Local women had set up their crafts between the produce booths and the small sidewalk cafés.

Nobody just talked—they shouted. They yelled their opinions. They laughed. Hands and arms were used as punctuation, and Tory loved it. She felt alarmingly alive as she walked beside the man who held her life in his hands.

Marc was going to find Alex. Tory's heart pounded as she tightened her hand around his. She might never see Marc Savin again but she would remember this day forever.

Marc glanced down at her. "Okay?"

Tory nodded, melting against him as he pulled her close for a hug. Her fingers clutched the linen jacket as she looked up at him. "Is someone watching us again?"

"A couple of hundred someones." His voice was husky, and filled with amusement.

"You'd better kiss me, then."

"Yes. I think I had better do just that." He leaned against the wall and pressed his mouth to hers with a sweetness and tenderness that made her go limp.

"Do you think they've gone now?" she asked a little breathlessly as his head moved away and he looked down at her with a bemused expression.

He didn't even bother to look over her shoulder as he said huskily, "One more kiss should about do it." And bent back to his task.

They could have been alone on the planet, for all Tory knew, as she closed her eyes and leaned into him, feeling the warmth of his mouth on hers. When he eventually stopped they were both breathing hard. Marc took her hand as they moved back into the crowd.

They paused to watch an old woman with arthritic fingers make lace as delicate as a cobweb. Tory would have loved to linger to buy some of the fine work, but Marc drew her away.

They had strolled several yards before Marc told her to wait, and he moved back through the crowd. Moments later he returned with a whisper-fine lace scarf, bought from the old woman.

Tory's eyes lit up as she took the creamy fabric from his hand. "Oh, Marc. Thank you. It's absolutely beautiful."

"Drape it over your arm," he said tightly. "It'll help hide the cast."

And Tory hid her hurt, draping the lace over her right arm and hugging it against her body. What had she expected, for heaven's sake? That he'd bought her a present as a token of his esteem? She had to concentrate on what she was here for—to rescue her brother.

Alex, where are you? she thought desperately, again following closely behind Marc as he pushed through the crowd.

Marc bought her a huge piece of coconut from a vendor and she ate it while they strolled away from the piazza and down one of the myriad side streets. Here the houses cast the narrow streets in deep shadow, making it marginally cooler. Tory finished the coconut and Marc waited as she went to a wall fountain to wash her hands.

Marc saw how rigid her back was and cursed himself. He hadn't been able to resist buying that scrap of lace. Her eyes had shone for a moment when he'd given it to her. But, damn it, he couldn't have her believing this was just a little vacation.

The life of one of his best agents was hanging by a thread. If they didn't find Lynx soon, it might be too late.

Victoria wiped her hand on her leggings and started walking toward him. She stopped in midstride, her head jerking up, the color draining from her face.

He took a step in her direction, then halted without touching her. "Victoria? What is it?" Her eyes were glazed as she stared blankly over his head. He was about to shake her when he realized what was happening.

Victoria had found her brother.

She stood frozen in place. He was afraid to touch her lest he break the communication.

Marc swiftly scanned the narrow alley. Water splashed into the verdigris basin beside him, misting his arm with cool water. The noise of the hundreds of people crowding the piazza a few blocks away was muted, the street shadowy. Thank God there was no one in sight.

He ached to hold her, but his hands clenched into tight fists as she swayed slightly. He was in big trouble.

She was a major weakness at a time when he could least afford any mistakes. He hadn't worked with a partner since Krista, and she'd been an experienced agent. Victoria was a civilian. But he'd had to bring her along to expedite the release of Lynx as quickly as possible. And he hadn't forgotten that he'd also brought her in the event that if she was part of a conspiracy, he would be able to keep an eye on her.

He'd had no intention of getting within ten feet of Victoria Jones. Unfortunately he'd miscalculated badly. If it had been pure lust, he could have dealt with it. Unfortunately that wasn't the case.

Victoria brought out a tender side of him he'd never known. There was something about her that got under his skin; something that tugged at that secret place he'd buried and forgotten long ago.

He leaned back against the rough wall, keeping his eyes moving constantly to make sure she was safe. She was so vulnerable, especially now.

He wished to God she'd snap out of her trance so he could get her safely back to the grotto. The angle of the sun indicated that considerable time had passed as they had wandered through the market.

He reached out a steadying hand when he saw her jolt, as if waking from hypnosis. "Are you all right?"

Victoria blindly felt for his hand, and Marc encircled her with his arms, pulling her against him. Holding him tightly, she pressed her face against his shirt. He could feel the warmth of her tears soaking his shirt; but she cried silently, her body barely moving.

Tilting her face up with his finger, he scanned her still-pale skin. "You don't have time to fall apart. Do you hear me, Victoria? No time, princess." He hardened his heart as she looked up at him with eyes awash with fresh tears. "Give me the where and what, and you're on your way back to camp."

She swallowed several times, dashing her fingertips across her cheek. "He's being held at the Palazzo Visconti." She stepped away from him to dip her hand into the fountain and scrub at her face. Her voice was flat and devoid of any emotion. "Only one man is guarding him now. But there are more than twenty upstairs in the palace."

Marc's eyes narrowed. "Upstairs? Don't tell me—"

"I thought Alex said 'dungeon'—" Tory looked up at him. "Surely I must have misunderstood."

"'Fraid not, princess." Marc was grim. "Palazzo Visconti was built in the early 1400s, complete with a moat and dungeons." He frowned. "Did you get anything else?"

Victoria ran the fragmented "dialogue" through her mind to get it straight. "He says there is a secret door into the palace from the park—but there are motion detectors on all the other entrances. The public isn't allowed to visit the royal suites, and that's where Spider is." Tory grimaced. "I'm not even going to ask. Alex says he has a couple of broken ribs and the perfect nose you always ragged him about will never be the same. They change the guards irregularly, they do a lot of drinking after ten, and seem to be pretty lax." Victoria chewed her lip. "Marc, Alex said to tell you to be especially careful. Someone inside wants you badly enough to have set this whole thing up. Alex said they are waiting for you but . . . but you have no face. Does that make any sense?"

"It's what I was expecting," he replied, his tone grim. "Did Lynx tell you anything else?"

"He believes the bird can still fly." Victoria frowned as Marc urged her back the way they had come, bending to pick up the scrap of lace that had slipped from her arm. "What 'bird'? A helicopter?"

"Yeah." Marc grinned. "The Hughes 500 chopper that Lynx flew in. We thought we'd lost it. The Huey. . . Damn, that's great! At least we have one piece of good news. It sure beats waiting around for Angelo. With the helicopter in commission we can fly out."

"Where are we going now?" Tory draped the lacy fabric over her cast and walked faster to keep up with his long strides.

She tried to read his expression, but his face was suddenly shuttered as he lost the smile and his jaw tightened. "I'll take you back to the truck. Your part in this is over."

"Oh, but . . ."

Marc turned and pinned her in place, his fingers like a vise around her upper arm. "You go back to the grotto, no ifs, ands or buts about it. Got that?" His mouth was hard and his fingers tightened until she nodded. "Don't try and play the hero, Victoria. I'll get your brother out. By this time tomorrow, Marezzo will just be a memory."

She tried to pull her arm out of his grasp. "You're hurting me."

"Not as much as those sons of bitches will if they catch up with you again." He dropped his hand from her arm, surprising her as he flung his arm around her waist and pulled her close to his side. "Keep close, keep you mouth shut and walk."

Victoria didn't have much choice. The square was still crowded and noisy, and the press of people and Marc's arm kept them as close together as Siamese twins. "I hate to bring this up, but I'm starving."

"You should have eaten this morning."

"I want real food." Tory glanced up at him as they had to pause to let one of the vendors, pulling a cart piled high with produce, go by.

As soon as their path was clear, Marc stopped and bought her a square of pizza. He waited while the vendor rolled it in paper and handed it to her.

"Are you sure you can find your way back?"

Victoria's mouth watered at the savory aroma of garlic and tomato. "Yes, I can find my way back." She saw the way he scanned each face in the crowd. "In fact, I can even find my way back to the truck on my own. Go ahead." She could feel his impatience as he tightened his hand around her waist. "It's not helping Alex if you have to waste time leading me about when I'm perfectly capable on my own."

They'd come to the wide gate and Tory turned to look up at him. "The truck's right over there, I'll be fine."

For a moment he looked as if he was going to say something, but Tory put her fingers against his lips. "I'm a big girl. Go. Be careful," she said softly, standing on her tiptoes to kiss his unsmiling mouth. Before he could respond, she turned and walked away.

She could feel his eyes boring into her back and knew the moment when he turned and walked behind the high walls of the city.

It was so hot, and her heart pounded as Tory hurried toward the battered vehicle. Marc would get Alex out. She knew that.

It wasn't until she eased between the ancient pickup and the wine truck that she saw the man. He was leaning against the passenger door of the wine truck, and she'd have to squeeze past him to open her door.

He was about her height but wiry, with bulging muscles and brown eyes that surveyed her up and down. Tory shivered despite the heat. He looked like trouble. She wished she'd let Marc escort her.

For an instant she considered going back around her vehicle and climbing in through the passenger door. The man took a drag on his cigarette and flicked it into the dirt at his feet. Smoke spiraled from his nose and his eyes narrowed as she paused.

Tory glanced over her shoulder as she heard the whisper of footsteps in the sand behind her. Another man stood there, barring her retreat.

She recognized the second man and a shudder rippled through her body: Giorgio had been one of the two men who had held her in Pescarna. The hot metal of the truck pressed into her shoulder blades. The man who had tossed down his cigarette moved toward her, and Giorgio effectively blocked her way from behind. The pizza she'd been holding dropped to the ground unnoticed. Tory glanced from one to the other. She desperately forced the air in and out of her lungs.

Think Victoria. Don't panic.

"Buon giorno, Signorina Jones." Giorgio moved between the trucks until he was just an arm's length away from her. "You have met Mario. Yes?" Tory recoiled from the smell of garlic on his breath and the stink of old sweat that permeated the still-hot air.

Of the two, Giorgio was a known quantity and therefore the most dangerous. She shot a glance at the other man, hoping she could evoke some sense of chivalry. She'd never seen such cold brown eyes. Okay, no help there.

She was trapped between the two vehicles and effectively cornered by her two assailants. For a moment she considered hurling herself into the bed of the truck. The sides were just too high and Giorgio and Mario were closing in.

Could she attack them if they came any closer? With what? She wished she had one of Marc's nasty-looking guns. A knife would have been good. She didn't even have a toothpick, for God's sake.

If only...

Her arm thumped against the wheel well. Wait a moment, she *did* have a weapon—of sorts. The heavy plaster cast!

Tory tried a smile. She hoped to God it looked more natural than it felt.

The man on her left grinned back, showing large yellow teeth. "You come back for Giorgio, yes?"

"Ah." Tory frantically glanced back and forth between the two men. The market was still crowded with people. Surely if she stalled these two long enough, someone would come out and help her. "I didn't get to see Pavina last time," she said weakly. "It's very interesting, isn't it? Did you go to market today?"

Oh, God, she sounded like a babbling idiot. Her shoulders ached from pressing against the truck. Her braid, still hooked under her shirt in back, made a lump that chafed at her skin. She could feel the sweat running down her sides and trickling down her face. The salt stung her eyes, but she was too terrified to blink.

"You come with Giorgio now."

Victoria shook her head. "No, thank you, I have to go. I'm meeting a friend and he'll be worried about me." She hated the way her voice shook. Still no one was coming to her aid. Somehow she was going to have to extricate herself from these men and get away.

With surprisingly steady legs she moved toward Mario. "It was interesting meeting you, but I really have to go now." Tory came abreast of him. She gave him a weak smile, her heart pumping as she moved past him, managing to grab the door handle.

Lord, I did it!

Yanking the handle down she pulled at the door. It stuck and she pulled harder. As the door flew open, she felt a hand grab her hair. Her scalp stung as Giorgio gripped her braid, his fingers tight against her neck. Her eyes stung and the baseball cap fell unheeded to the ground.

"*Signorina* will come now." He pulled at the braid until it was free of her shirt, twisting it around his beefy wrist, jerking it so her head was tilted back painfully. Tears of rage blurred her vision as Tory struggled against his grip.

"*Andiamo!*" Garlic breath seared her face as he spat the command. She had no idea what he'd said, but he was pulling her inexorably toward the back of the truck.

Tory kicked him; he merely laughed, calling to Mario in Italian as he dragged her backward. She managed to roll her head, sinking her teeth into Giorgio's wrist.

Snarling an oath, Giorgio tightened his grip on her hair. Tory didn't feel the pain. Her jaw ached as she held on for dear life while he talked furiously to Mario.

A steely arm slammed across her throat as Mario lifted her easily off her feet. She dangled helplessly between the two men.

Her jaw seemed locked, despite the arm across her windpipe. Lights danced before her eyes as the arm across her throat pressed harder. She wanted to draw in a lungful of air, but she knew if she relaxed they would take her.

Giorgio fired a command in Italian at Mario, who immediately pinched her nose between foul-smelling fingers. Tory's jaw unclamped as she sucked in great drafts of burning air through her mouth.

The metallic taste of blood was on her tongue and she spat it out. Right on Giorgio's fancy handmade shoes. She hung limply in Mario's arms, his forearm still across her throat as she struggled to breathe.

The hand pressed over her nose made breathing impossible. Dizzy and faint, Tory forced her body to remain limp. She was beyond terrified. Death was preferable to what she knew Giorgio was capable of doing to her. Oh, God. She couldn't go through that again. She just couldn't!

Without warning she lashed out, both legs coming up and hitting Giorgio in the stomach, and he fell backward with a cry. Mario, who was still holding her, started backing up in surprise, pulling Tory with him as Giorgio staggered to his feet. She jerked out of his grip and swung her right arm up. Her cast hit Giorgio across the nose with a satisfying crunch. Pain shot up her arm. Blood spurted from the man's broken nose.

Victoria then used her knee with all her strength and Mario went down like a tree, his hands cupping his groin.

Leaping over his crouched body, Tory ran for the open door of the truck. Sliding across the seat she fumbled with the door latch with her cast and frantically searched under the seat for the key.

The door wouldn't lock. Straightening, she used her good hand to try to force down the little chrome button, her heart in her throat. She leaned over and slammed down the button on the passenger side, but the driver's side wouldn't lock, no matter how hard she tried.

She still couldn't locate the key. Peering through the grimy window, she saw Giorgio shaking his head, blood still spurting from his nose, as he lumbered between the vehicles toward her.

Where's the key? Where the hell is that key? Tory ran frantic fingers under the seat again and again. The key was gone.

Sliding across the seat, Tory managed to unlock and fling open the passenger door. She catapulted out and took off at a dead run. There was an open field to her left. Beyond that a stand of trees that might offer some protection. If she could make it.

Not looking back, she sprinted for the field, her bangs stuck to her forehead wet with sweat. Her arm throbbed painfully. Within seconds, the force of a body cannoning into her from behind took her down, and she gasped in a mouthful of powdery dirt as she hit the ground.

Giorgio's body pinned her as Tory twisted and kicked, screaming for help as she tried to escape from beneath the knee he'd pressed into her back.

She was lying facedown, the weight of his body holding her firmly as she bucked and squirmed uselessly. With a punishing grip, he flipped her over on her back, his face contorting murderously. The cast was handy for another swat: Unfortunately, this time it only connected with the side of his head. He roared his rage.

Fatalistically, Tory saw his elbow lift. She closed her eyes tightly as his fist connected on her jaw with brutal force.

6

VICTORIA, OPEN YOUR EYES. Wake up. Now!

Alex? Victoria's eyes fluttered but refused to open. *Alex, are you . . . are you all right?*

Tory forced her eyes open and looked around. She rotated her jaw. It ached.

She could hear his amusement in her mind. *Honey, I'm fine. Let's concentrate on you, okay? Where are you hurt? Can you move?*

Where are we?

The bowels of the earth, at the "hotel" Palazzo Visconti. His tone was rueful and bitter. *Can you see anything?*

The room was about ten feet by ten feet. Stained blocks of stone formed the walls, floor and ceiling. The only furniture was the bed she was lying on—a bare dirty mattress that was cold and damp with mildew and other things she didn't want to identify.

There was a tiny window high in the wall above the bed that let in a little of dusk's meager light. It was certainly too high to reach and too small to crawl through even if she could. She stifled a groan.

Tory, Alex's voice was near, but she still had to close her eyes to concentrate because he sounded weak. *How badly are you hurt?*

She moved her jaw again, cautiously. It hurt, as well it should after the punch she'd taken from Giorgio's fist. Her broken arm throbbed under the cast. *No major problems.* There was absolutely no point in having Alex worry needlessly.

Tory heard a door open and close nearby. She squinted at the door to her cell. Constructed of heavy dark wood, raw and stained with hundreds of years of moisture, it was banded by wide metal strips. Very old but with a depressingly modern-looking locking device.

Alex?

She shifted restlessly on the narrow straw-filled cot. What had happened to Alex?

She mentally called his name several times before she felt him inside her head again. *What happened?* she asked frantically.

They are coming your way. They think I'm your boyfriend and they want Marc. Do you hear me, Tory? They want Phantom.... Don't tell them.

Tory heard loud noises coming from down the hall where she knew Alex was being held and heard the key grate in the lock on her door.

She was paralyzed with fear as three men came into the room, shutting the door behind them. "Good evening, Miss Jones."

She had only seen Christoph Ragno once when she was being held in Pescarna. The memory would live with her for the rest of her life. Tory swallowed the bile threatening to choke her. "Why was I brought here?" she demanded in a tone that reminded her of her grandmother. "I want to see the American consul. You have no right to kidnap an American tourist like this."

"You have no rights here, Miss Jones. I thought I had made that perfectly obvious the last time you visited Marezzo."

Tory forcibly pushed the memories aside, biting down hard on her lip to ground herself. Coward or not, she had to keep her head. Alex was close by and Marc was sure to figure out where she was. All she had to do was keep as calm as possible and not incite this man to violence.

Ragno's head was too big for his body. His greasy hair could have been blond and clung thinly to his pink scalp, and he had ears like sugar-bowl handles. His face was florid and shiny. Tory couldn't control the tremor that raced up her spine as his light brown eyes seemed to touch her skin.

"You had no right to detain me last time and even less so, now. You know that I'm—"

"I believe you already know Giorgio and Mario?" His lips stretched into a gruesome smile over large teeth as he glanced at the other two men standing against the door.

Tory spared an unsympathetic glance at Giorgio's swollen nose. Mario shot her a murderous look.

"What are you doing back on Marezzo, Miss Jones? I thought you had enough of our hospitality the last time you visited?"

"I never did finish my vacation," Tory said calmly, her insides shaking at the menace in his eyes.

"We have your lover, Miss Jones," Ragno announced in a sibilant voice that grated on her nerves.

Oh, good Lord. They had found Marc. Tory felt faint and pressed her legs against the sharp edge of the metal bed frame behind her.

"He also says that he arrived in Marezzo for a vacation." Ragno assessed her, his watery brown eyes sharp. "He, of course, has been enjoying our hospitality for several months, awaiting your arrival."

Victoria could have cried with relief. He was talking about Alex! She tilted her chin. "If some man said he's my lover, then he lied to you. I came here on my own. I arrived this morning from Naples."

Victoria screamed as he grabbed her hair and wrenched her head up, exposing her throat. He held a small sharp razor against her cheek.

"Stop lying, bitch! There was no flight from Naples today."

She stared at his face, inches from hers as he twisted her hair in his fist, and tears smarted in her eyes. "I . . . I came on the mail boat." Oh, God, she prayed that the mail boat had arrived this morning.

She felt his hand relax slightly against her head, and she winced as he pulled her up close to his soft body. "I'll check on that." Still gripping her hair in his fist, he jerked his head at Mario. The other man nodded and slipped from the room.

The razor came up against her cheek again, icy cold as he pressed it to her face. She felt cold sweat bathe her skin. "Where is Phantom, Miss Jones?"

Tory looked blankly at him. "Phantom? Who . . ."

He slapped her. Hard. "Tell me where Phantom is! Now!" Spittle sprayed her face as he yelled. She flinched before his hand arced and he slapped her again, hauling her up as she slumped sideways.

Tory sobbed. "I don't know what you want. I don't know anyone called Phan—"

He hit her again, holding her head still as he wound the yard of hair in his fist.

Her head reeled and her face throbbed as she felt darkness closing in. Releasing her hair, he grabbed the front of her T-shirt, and holding her still, he brought the razor down with a terrifying stroke that slashed the cloth from neck to hem.

Tory staggered backward as he held the sharp instrument up. "I'll give you one hour to regain your memory, Miss Jones. Then I'll let Giorgio pay you back for your little dance in the parking lot. Giorgio isn't as fond of the ladies as I am, are you, Gio? Or perhaps you'd prefer Mario? I know he would like to prove to you that he is still very much the man."

He shoved her—hard. She hit the bed, sinking into the filthy mattress and gasping for breath, her ears ringing from the blow.

In the dim recesses of her mind, she could hear Alex's voice telepathically calling her name. She pushed him away with her last scrap of strength. Her eyes locked on the pale shiny face of Ragno as he stood over her.

Tory's whole body shook as he leaned closer and trailed the razor down the bare skin exposed by the slashed shirt. "I enjoy playing as much as the next man, Miss Jones." Ragno's loathsome voice snaked across her skin as he leaned in, close to her face. "Obviously, Giorgio didn't warn you sufficiently on your last visit. I can assure you that I have absolutely no compunction about the methods I'll use to make you talk. I'll give you one hour to tell me where he is.

Straightening, he jerked his head at Giorgio and the two men shut the door behind them. Tory heard the rasp of the key in the lock from the outside, and she cradled her hot cheek in her shaking hand.

She crouched on the bed, too weak to stand, staring unseeingly at the door. She shook so badly that she couldn't stay upright, and she allowed her body to roll back on the bed. Curling into a fetal position, she felt the tears course down her face as she sobbed uncontrollably.

"Victoria!"

Alex! She couldn't let him know. He would be mad with rage.

"Damn it, Tory, answer me. Right now!"

She sat up, jamming her hand against her mouth to stop the jerky sobs she couldn't prevent. And she blocked her thoughts as hard as she could until she was calmer.

"I'm all right." She managed, moments later. The lie held barely a tremor.

"What did those bastards do to you?"

"Ragno knows that Marc's here. Oh, God, Alex. He knows."

"Calm down. He doesn't know anything. Do you hear me, Tory? He doesn't know squat. He was fishing and hoping, but he doesn't know about Marc."

"They are coming back in an hour to get me.... Alex, I hate this."

"I know you do, precious." Alex's warm comforting voice came through loud and clear. *"Did you have time to tell Marc everything I told you?"*

"Yes."

Relief bathed his words as he said calmly, *"Then he'll come for us. Get yourself together and try to calm down. Can you do that, Tory?"*

"What's the alternative?"

"That's my girl." Alex gave a rusty laugh. *"Just hang in there."*

She was "hanging in there" an hour later when the door opened. In the pitch-dark room, she had to squint into the light from the hallway. Her heart sank to her toes when she saw the bulky outline of Giorgio.

The dim lighting couldn't conceal the malevolent gaze directed at her over the swollen flesh of his broken nose. "Boss wants you. Upstairs."

Clutching her ripped shirt between her fingers, Tory gave him a wide berth as she went through the door.

She'd managed to close the two pieces of fabric over her bra and belt it tightly around her waist so that she was marginally covered. She shot him a dirty look when he leered at the exposed swell of her breasts as she passed him.

"Right," he instructed, walking behind her. Tory obediently turned right down the stone corridor. She felt Alex two doors away, and drew strength from his thoughts.

The air was stifling. Hot and humid and heavy to breathe as Tory stumbled ahead of her guard. The flashlight he held illuminated only a few feet in front of her and she stumbled on the uneven floor.

"Left," he directed.

She turned when Giorgio said, "Turn," walked up steps on command and kept her back ramrod straight. She was sick to death of macho men. She *hated* adventure. Particularly *this* adventure.

There was light ahead and Giorgio turned off the flashlight.

"Walk." He pushed her ahead of him with the flashlight. Tory wanted to smash his broken nose and have the satisfaction of hearing him scream again. She tilted her chin and kept her eyes fixed firmly ahead.

A ten-foot-high elaborately carved mahogany door stood closed before her. She moved aside and waited while he opened it, then cautiously stepped into the room.

A magnificent Persian carpet, in shades of cream and burgundy, stretched over a white marble floor. As Giorgio marched her across the carpet, she could see several black heel marks scuffed into the light-colored fibers.

Overhead was a frescoed ceiling. On the walls hung priceless paintings. Their elaborate gilt frames, however, were adorned with cobwebs, and the delicate brushwork was marred by dust and neglect. A magnificent gilded table stood against one wall, where a three-foot-high Venetian Glass vase held what must have been an artistic arrangement of cut flowers. Long-since dead, both leaves and petals were brittle and brown in piles on the tabletop thick with dust.

Their footsteps were muffled by the thickness of the carpet as they passed white Carrara marble statues and other incredible objets d'art, all of which needed dusting. Tory held back a sneeze.

At the far end of the room, seated on enormous burgundy velvet couches, sat three men. One to each sofa.

Giorgio prodded her back again as her footsteps lagged. The closer she got, the more Tory's apprehension grew. Her heart lodged in her throat, and her nerves were raw.

She recognized Ragno, but the other two men had their backs to her.

"Brung the girl," Giorgio said nasally. Ragno rose, his expression hidden from the men behind him. The pale hand he wrapped around Giorgio's upper arm trembled with fury. "Thank you, Giorgio," he said loudly, then continued in a furious undertone. "Your timing needs improving. Can't you see that we have unexpected company?" His sibilant voice sent a shiver up Tory's spine. She winced as his thick fingers dug into her bare arm.

His pink sausagelike fingers looked ridiculous holding a delicate crystal wineglass. He took a sip and looked at Giorgio over her shoulder.

"Did she give you any trouble?"

"No, sir."

"Good. You may wait outside the door."

Tory heard Giorgio's muffled footsteps as he walked away.

The fingers on her upper arm tightened. "Watch what you say, Miss Jones. If our visitor suspects anything unusual, you will both die."

Out of the corner of her eye she saw one of the men cross his legs. She kept her eyes warily on Christoph Ragno. His pink scalp shone dully, reflecting the light from the gigantic chandelier overhead.

Grasping her arm in what could look like a solicitous gesture, he led her toward the three couches. Tory's skin crawled at his touch, and she tried to pull her arm away. His fingers squeezed her upper arm warningly.

She heard a small choking noise and glanced down at the man seated on the sofa.

And almost fainted.

Marc!

His expression was politely blank as he inclined his head in greeting, but his pale eyes blazed with warning.

"Come and sit down, my dear Miss Jones, and let me introduce you to my companions."

Tory shrugged off Ragno's hand as he led her to a sofa. She sank down, and accepted a glass of wine. She was sure all three men could see the pulse throbbing in her throat. She dared not look at Marc, who sat across from her.

"This is Samuel Hoag." Tory turned a stiff neck and looked at the other man. He was tall and painfully thin, with black hair that was parted neatly on one side. A small mustache cut across his thin upper lip, giving him a sinister, movie-villain look. She righted her wineglass as it slipped on her knee. There was something repulsively hypnotic about him.

His eyes, behind rimless glasses, looked deceptively benign as he stared back at her without so much as a greeting. He had enormous pale hands that stuck out of his jacket sleeves like Ichabod Crane's.

Tory shivered, the stem of the glass pressed into her palm.

"And this is our new friend, Sir Ian Spenser." Marc toasted her with his wineglass, his face bland.

"Charmed to meet you. Miss Jones, is it?" His British accent was so plummy it belonged in a Christmas pudding. Tory took a hasty sip of wine and choked back hysterical, terrified laughter.

She had absolutely no idea where or how Marc had procured the fabulous suit he wore. It was expensive and Italian designed, in a light weight fabric that flattered his long legs and hung beautifully from his broad shoulders. A slim gold watch was barely visibly beneath the correct half-inch of white Egyptian-cotton cuff. The finishing touch was a conservative old school tie.

He looked absolutely, mouth-wateringly wonderful. He also looked slightly bored as he sipped his wine and watched her as he would a stranger.

Tory didn't want to know what was going through Marc's mind as he looked at her bashed-up face and ripped T-shirt. She wondered just how Ragno was going to explain her odd appearance to "Sir Ian."

Ragno cleared his throat noisily in the silence. "Sir Ian will be our guest tonight. He came to see his old school friend, Prince Draven Visconti, who is vacationing in America this month with his family. Unfortunate that you missed each other, Sir Ian."

"Most unfortunate, old chap." Unfortunate indeed, considering that the prince had been assasinated several months ago. Marc rose to go to the bar, "May I?" His pant leg brushed Tory's ankle as he strolled by her. "More wine, Miss . . . Jones?" He held up the decanter, pouring his own before turning to the other two men when she mutely shook her head. She'd seen the nerve ticking in his jaw as he walked past her.

He was mad as fire, and Tory didn't have to be a mind reader to figure that out. The last person he was expecting to see here was her. Well, wasn't that just too bad! She certainly would have preferred being back at camp waiting, too!

Samuel Hoag sat stiffly in the corner of his sofa, his long legs stretched out. She fixed her eyes on the pale, hairless skin of his shin above his socks.

Hoag said, "No more wine," in a curiously mellifluous voice, while Ragno accepted, allowing Marc to refill his glass.

"Miss Jones was in a small accident at the marketplace this afternoon," Ragno said, smoothly accounting for her appearance. Savoring the wine, he shot Tory a warning look. "Mr. Hoag and I felt it best to offer her our hospitality in the absence of the royal family.

"I'm sure the princess has something suitable for you to wear for dinner, Miss Jones." He looked at her torn shirt with distaste. He called for Giorgio.

"Take Miss Jones to the family suite," he directed. "See that she is suitably dressed for dinner."

Tory managed not to look at Marc as she was removed from the room. But she could feel his gaze burning into her back.

When Giorgio opened the double doors, she noticed a man standing sentry outside—a blond version of Giorgio, with a gun holstered on his hip. The guard glanced curiously at her, and she edged her way past him, following Giorgio up a narrow circular stone stairway and along a dimly lit corridor.

The farther along they went, the more elaborate and elegant the furnishings became. They turned a corner and Giorgio gestured toward a gilt-and-ivory inlaid door.

"Princess's room." He took her arm, opened the door and roughly pushed her into the room.

She glanced over her shoulder as she shrugged his hand away. "How's your nose?" she asked with false sweetness.

He backed up, his fingers tenderly touching the grotesque swelling, and narrowed his eyes malevolently. "Signore Ragno said get dressed." He walked backward to the door, as if he had to watch her every movement. "Get dressed," he warned. "I'll come back to get you."

"Don't hurry back on my account," Tory said to the closed door, as she heard the key turn in the lock.

She made mental contact with Alex to let him know what was going on, then did a quick inventory of the room.

It was quite beautiful, decorated in shades of lavender and purple with accents of white. Like the room downstairs, it was covered with a thick layer of dust, and the once-fresh flowers were dead and crumbling.

Tory caught a glimpse of herself in the full-length mirror and groaned. Her hair was a wild, tangled mess, her jaw sported the bruise from Giorgio's fist, and her cheeks were streaked with dirt and tears.

She headed for the opulent gold-and-white-marble bathroom. Filling the enormous tub would take up half her allotted time, but she didn't care. After sprinkling violet-scented crystals into the churning water, she went back into the bedroom to find something to wear.

When Giorgio opened the door a short time later, without knocking, Tory was ready. She'd washed and dried her hair and used the hot rollers she'd found on the dressing table. The princess's gigantic walk-in closet was filled with fabulous clothes for all occasions.

Victoria had wasted precious moments pulling out a few pieces of casual clothing, and hiding them for later. Then her fingers had lingered on several stunning evening dresses.

It was irrational, she knew, under the circumstances, but she wanted Marc to see her in something sophisticated, something . . . sexy. The dress she chose was probably for some formal state function. With apologies to the absent princess, Tory had managed to pour herself into the dress and pull up the short zipper at the back just as Giorgio walked in.

"Dinner's ready." He'd changed into an ill-fitting suit that was too tight for his lumpy body, and he stared at her unblinkingly out of swollen eyes.

"Lead on, Macduff," Tory said as she pulled on the shoes and picked up the sheer silk scarf she'd tossed on the bed earlier, draping it over her arm.

Giorgio gave her a blank look and gestured for her to precede him. They turned right instead of left this time and continued down an endless corridor, their footsteps muffled by the thick runner.

She caught a glimpse of herself in an enormous mirror at the top of the stairs. The heavily beaded emerald silk gown clung to her body as if it had been painted on. The low-cut, square neckline exposed more of her breasts than was wise, and she could feel her hair caressing her bare back. The billowing sleeves were caught at the wrist with elastic, effectively hiding most of her grimy cast. As she passed the mirror she realized with a sinking heart that while the dress had seemed deceptively modest in the bedroom, when she walked she exposed her leg to the thigh.

She stopped dead at the top of the wide staircase. She must be out of her mind! What had she been thinking about when she'd selected this particular gown? Marc, that's who.

The last thing she wanted to do was let those men see her like this. Tory quickly turned away from the staircase, almost coming nose to nose with Giorgio, who was right behind her.

He pulled his gun out from under his jacket and leveled it at her chest. "Down."

"I have to change," Tory said firmly, swallowing her heart as he motioned her down the stairs with the deadly weapon.

"Down."

"Look," Tory tried, tiredly. "I'll take two seconds to find something else and be right back."

"Down." He pushed the gaping mouth of the pistol at the swell of her breasts, and Tory saw in his eyes how much he would love to pull the trigger.

He was the same height as she was in heels, and she was tempted to call his bluff, but one look at his dark eyes discouraged that idea. She sighed and took the first step down the red-carpeted stairs, holding on to the marble banister for balance.

Between the tightness and weight of the blasted dress and the unfamiliar high heels, she was liable to roll down the staircase and break her neck, so she made her way cautiously into the enormous foyer.

Giorgio grunted at a man standing outside the double doors. The guard swung the door open to the dining room, not bothering to hide the rifle resting over his arm. Tory shivered, tossing the ends of the sheer scarf over her shoulders so that it draped in front, effectively covering her cleavage.

The three men stood as Giorgio led her into the room. A painting the size of a small house adorned one wall. It was a breathtaking depiction of Palazzo Visconti before roads and modern civilization had blotted out the landscape.

The cherry-wood dining table probably seated more than fifty people. The three men, still standing, were at the far end. Great. Tory drew in a deep breath, raised her chin and started walking.

"Miss Jones, how nice of you to join us." Christoph Ragno pulled out the chair beside him, and Tory gratefully sank into it, looking straight into Marc's eyes across the table.

For a moment she saw blazing heat before he picked up the fluted Baccarat glass beside his place setting and took a sip, his face bland.

"You found things to your satisfaction, I trust?" Tory hated the sibilance of Ragno's voice.

"Everything was quite satisfactory. No, thank you," she added, putting her hand over her glass as he held up the bottle of wine.

"You don't drink, Miss Jones?" Marc asked politely, accepting a refill. He looked devastatingly handsome in a black tuxedo and crisp white shirt. The diamond earring was back, flashing in his ear, and his hair was tied back. He looked exactly the way he sounded—sophisticated, wealthy, British and slightly bored. For a moment his pewter gaze rested hotly on her breasts filmed by the sheer silk.

She forced herself to respond lightly. "Not on an empty stomach, Sir Ian." She realized she was fidgeting with the silverware and dropped her hands into her lap, managing to shrug enough of her hair over her shoulder to cover more of her chest.

"Your face seems to be swollen, Miss Jones," Marc said mildly. "You must have taken a nasty spill this afternoon." If Tory hadn't jerked her head up to look at him, she would have missed the way his tanned fingers tightened on the stem of his glass and the way his lips thinned.

"Let's just say I came into contact with an immovable object." She could feel the heat of Ragno's warning hand on her silk-clad knee. She twisted her legs out of reach and took a sip of water, giving him a furious glance over her glass.

God, would this never end? Beneath the thin veneer of civilization at the table, the tension in the room could have been cut with a knife. Ragno and Hoag had no idea who Marc really was, she was sure of that. But by the same token she could see that they were both wary of him. Marc appeared mildly bored by the whole thing—unless one caught a glimpse of his eyes, which were simmering with rage every time he looked at her. What was he going to do? How on earth was he going to manage to get both her and Alex out right under the noses of these men?

A white-uniformed waiter entered the room, and Tory felt the rumble of her stomach. She was absolutely starving, and she wondered how her body could still function as if everything were normal.

The food was beautiful to look at and absolutely inedible. The chef might be doing his job, but it was obviously under duress. While she tried to eat what tasted like pure salt, she listened to Marc telling the other two men of his friendship with the absent prince. He talked easily of his business interests in England and Europe. If she hadn't known better, she would have believed every word. His impersonation was impeccable.

Far from filling the empty void in her stomach, the food, either tasteless or so highly seasoned that she had to gulp her water, had settled like a ball into the nervous knot of her stomach.

The three men didn't seem to notice that she sat silently without contributing to the conversation. Outwardly, everything seemed surrealistically normal. Conversation flowed, wine was poured, courses served and plates removed and replaced.

It was with enormous relief that Tory saw the last dish taken away, and Ragno suggested brandy in the drawing room.

Marc rounded the table and took her elbow as they preceded the other two men out of the dining room. Tory's heels clicked on the white marble, and she was incredibly grateful for his support as they entered the formal drawing room. Her legs felt like jelly, and her heart had taken up permanent residence in her throat.

"What the hell induced you to wear— For God's sake, keep your hair where it is, covering your chest!" Marc gritted under his breath as he led her to a white velvet camelback sofa, his back to the other two. "And smile, damn it!"

Tory managed a credible smile, her heart in her eyes as she arranged her hair so that it pooled in her lap, and the long skirt so that it covered her knees.

Marc settled himself beside her, pinching the knees of his pants and leaning back as if he didn't have a care in the world. Tory felt perspiration beading her forehead under her bangs.

The other two men took the sofa opposite and Ragno indicated the tarnished, Georgian silver coffee service on the table between them. "Will you pour, Miss Jones?"

Tory shifted on the down-filled cushion, starting as she felt Marc's fingers in her hair. She shot him a startled glance as he pushed her hair back from her face.

"You have glorious hair, Miss Jones. I'd hate to see it trailing in the coffee." For a moment, as their eyes locked, they might have been the only two people in the room.

Marc felt the familiar heat when he touched her. It was an incredible risk that could blow his cover, but ever since she'd walked into the dining room, his fingers had itched to tangle in the glossy dark curls that flowed down her back and over the tantalizing swell of her breasts.

She avoided looking at him as she handed him his cup. Her face was pale, the swelling of her jaw an obscenity on her clear skin, despite the makeup. Marc vowed he would kill the bastard who had hit her.

She was incredibly beautiful in that figure-hugging green dress, her hair shiny and wildly curling down her back, her eyes shadowed. How on God's earth he'd ever thought her plain was a mystery.

He let out a short frustrated breath and caught Samuel Hoag's assessing glance across the table. Marc shrugged as if to say, *I find her attractive. Why not?*

He knew he was playing a dangerous game. He had to get Lynx out. Tory's brother wouldn't be any possible help with a couple of busted ribs and a broken nose. First things first. Get Lynx and then get Tory the hell out of here.

He studied the two men and mentally tallied everything he knew about them while keeping up his end of the conversation. Out of the corner of his eye he saw the way Victoria's body seemed to slump against the pillows. She jerked upright and settled the cup back in its saucer, pushing her hair out of the way as she straightened her spine. He almost smiled as she tilted that combative little chin.

She must be tired as hell. They had been up since the crack of dawn. She'd barely eaten anything at dinner and she'd been to hell and back today. She was holding up remarkably well, he thought, as he drank the strong coffee, and he felt a surge of pride. She'd gone along with his "Sir Ian" cover, but she was exhausted and off-balance enough to blow the whole thing. He needed to get her out of the room. Noticing the subtle tremor in her hands as she clutched the delicate cup, he said mildly, "It seems Miss Jones is about to fall asleep in her coffee." Marc rose and held out his hand to her, seeing the glaze of exhaustion in her eyes. "Allow me to escort you to your room, my dear."

Tory took hold of his strong fingers like a lifeline. "Thank you . . . I do have a bit of a headache."

"Giorgio will see her upstairs, Sir Ian. No need for you to bother yourself," Ragno interjected smoothly, snapping his fingers while pinning Marc with a warning look.

Marc helped Tory to her feet and waited until Giorgio came alongside her. He gave her a small smile and seated himself, watching the sway of her hips in the tight dress as the other man led her away. Her clean, shining hair caught the lights from the overhead chandeliers as it tumbled down her back.

"A beautiful woman," Marc said, leaning over to refill his cup as the door closed behind her.

Ragno glanced at Hoag and then back at Marc. "The attraction seems mutual, but not particularly wise."

"Do you think so, old chap? How intriguing." Marc raised one dark brow with amusement. "I think I shall have to go up and check on Miss Jones's . . . headache."

Ragno's eyes went cold. "I wouldn't be too confident of my welcome if I were you, Sir Ian. Despite the way she was dressed this evening, Miss Jones does not give the impression she is a woman who intends to share her sexual favors with a man she has just met." He glanced over at Hoag. "We could perhaps procure a young lady from the village for Sir Ian, Samuel?"

Marc shot his cuffs as he rose, hiding his irritation with a cocky grin. "No need, old chap. Why send out for someone when I have what I want right here?" His smile widened as he murmured, "I think I'll just give it a go with my best shot. I say, are you a betting man, Ragno?"

7

TORY KICKED OFF HER high heels as soon as Giorgio left. She was absolutely exhausted, but the coffee was coursing through her system. She paced from one end of the opulent bedroom to the other before pulling at the zipper of her dress.

As she was shrugging the heavy gown over her shoulders she heard a brisk knock at the door and her heartbeat sped up again. Surely not Giorgio? He would have just barged in. For a moment she paused, holding the dress securely against her thumping heart.

"Miss Jones?"

Marc! Tory stumbled to the door, tugging at the Queen Anne chair she'd wedged under the handle. She pulled open the door and almost fell into his arms.

She was about to say his name, but he put his fingers over her mouth. "I found some aspirin in my room, Miss Jones. These should do the trick with that headache of yours. If you have a couple of glasses you can wash them down with this." He held up a bottle, and said under his breath, "Invite me in, damn it."

"That was very . . . kind of you. Please, come in." He still wore the tux but had stripped off his bow tie and loosened the collar of the white shirt. A wedge of dark skin covered with crinkly hair showed through the opening.

He followed her into the room, closing the door behind him. Tory stood next to the bed, her hand still over her chest to hold up the weight of the loosened dress.

"I know you said that you weren't a drinker, my dear." He nodded his approval of the chair by the door. "But I think a couple of these and a glass of good Italian wine will fix you right up. You should sleep like a baby."

"That's very kind of you, Sir . . . Sir Ian. I'll get the glasses." Tory watched Marc prowl the room and then turned to the bar and picked up a couple of crystal wineglasses.

"Thanks." Marc took both glasses and set them on the bedside table. He lifted the shade from the lamp and nodded before pouring the wine. "Here you go." He handed her one of the glasses and made a noisy production of opening the pill bottle. "Two of these should get rid of that headache." He mouthed the word *bugs* and indicated the lamp with a jerk of his shoulder. Tory's eyes opened wide.

Bugs? As in someone listening to their every word? She looked at Marc with a small question and he nodded grimly. "Keep talking!" he said under his breath, as he continued to check the rest of the room.

She couldn't think of a thing to say as she stared at him blankly. He held up three fingers and came back to her. His hand slipped under the silky fall of her hair.

How could he think of sex *now?* Tory moved away but he grabbed her by the arm and drew her back, close enough so that she felt the heat of his body.

"You have beautiful hair, my dear. When I saw you at dinner tonight, all I could think of was having it wrapped around my body." His voice was husky, his eyes held a warning. *"Say something encouraging, damn it!"*

She met his gaze, her mind totally blank. How could she hope to have two conversations at once, with his fingers stroking her neck? Tory closed her eyes and tilted her face. "Kiss me!" she demanded—to Marc *and* to their listening audience. She didn't care.

For a moment he paused and then with a muffled groan he took her offered mouth and kissed her hard. Tory wrapped her arms around his neck, straining to get closer as he used his lips and tongue to drive her out of her mind.

When he stepped away, the dress fell to the floor. Tory just stood there in her sheer stockings and lacy bra as Marc moved swiftly about the room, her breath was labored as he came back to her.

He stroked the swell of her breasts above the push-up bra and then shook his head. "You have a remarkable body, Miss Jones . . . Victoria, if I may? So soft, so smooth . . . Oh yes! Just like that! Is this an invitation?"

"Yes." Tory replied weakly as he pulled her over to the bed.

The springs creaked slightly as he pulled her down on the bed. A puff of dust settled, she bit her lip. The lavender satin spread felt cool on her heated skin. She started unbuttoning his shirt, desperate to feel his bare skin against hers. He held her hand away and shook his head.

"Let's get you out of this dress, shall we?" Goose bumps rose on her skin as he kissed her neck noisily. *"Where is Alex?"* She closed her eyes and wrapped her arms around his neck, pressing her face against his throat.

"In the dungeon, directly below this room."

"God, but you're responsive. Do that again, darling." He shifted so that the springs groaned, and used his teeth to nip at her neck until she moaned. His eyes filling with triumph, he whispered close to her ear, *"Six stories down."* His voice was grim. *"Where's the belt?"*

"The belt?"

Marc shook her so that the bedsprings creaked even harder. *"The belt, Tory. The belt. Where is it? Concentrate!* Would you like me to kiss you here? What about here, love?"

"I can't concentrate when you do that!" she hissed low against his throat.

He lifted his head to look at her. *"Your life could depend on making this sound good, Victoria."* She went cold as she remembered that two feet away, under the lampshade, was a listening device. Someone at the other end was hearing everything that went on in the room. She pushed her hair out of her face and nodded, her eyes dark. "Oh, yes. Kiss me there." Her voice shook with nervousness. *"On the chair under the window."*

"Keep making noise." He got up silently and went to the window, rummaging under her clothes until he found the belt he'd insisted she wear that morning. It felt like months ago. Tory sat up and curled her legs under her panty-clad bottom. Every now and then she jumped up and down a little and tried to make sexy noises. She felt absolutely ridiculous.

Marc came back and slid across the bed. Tunneling his fingers through her hair, he whispered at the side of her face, *"Can you communicate with Lynx and let him know what I'm doing?"*

Tory nodded. The bedsprings rang out as he moved rapidly and let out a satisfied moan. Tory almost giggled hysterically, but he shot her a warning look. "Ahh...do that again. No. Harder, darling. That's it!"

He moved cautiously to the end of the bed, lifting his leg onto the small upholstered bench at the foot. He raised his pant leg, and then motioned with his hand for her to keep moving.

Tory slithered around on the bed and made satisfied noises as she watched him pull a small eight-shot Sauer automatic pistol from his ankle holster.

"This damned bed is too soft," he said harshly. Pulling Victoria off the bed, he indicated the window.

"I don't mind the floor." Tory obediently followed him to the window.

"Tell Alex exactly what I'm doing." Marc pressed at a hidden device on the belt buckle and the backing opened. "God, woman, you're killing me." He checked the contents, pulling out a thin fishing line, which he

fixed to the buckle of the belt. Then he attached the gun to the line through the loop.

"Do you like this, darling?" Marc's husky voice was loud in the quiet room. Tory couldn't believe he could sound so aroused while performing totally unrelated tasks. She was finding it hard enough to concentrate on what to tell Alex. She scowled at him as he finished tying off the belt. "And this? *Answer me, for God's sake!*"

"Yes!" Tory hissed through clenched teeth. Marc opened the window quietly and started lowering the line down the outside wall.

"Tell Lynx to be watching his window. The belt and the Sauer are on their way down. Lift your hips, darling. There, that's it. Does that feel good?"

Tory shivered as cool night air rushed in through the open window. "Y-yes." She tried to focus on what she was telling Alex. Marc gave her whispered instructions for Alex, while making lovemaking noises as he carefully lowered the belt.

She couldn't forget that someone was listening to every word. Tory wrapped her arms around her shivering body, and the moan she supplied was heartfelt and very real—the breeze billowing through the sheer drapes was icy on her bare skin.

"He's got it," she whispered, as he pulled away and closed the window. *"He said he's as ready as he's ever been. He'll be waiting for you in two hours just like you said."*

"Good," Marc whispered back. *"Now, scream."*

Tory looked blank. *"Scream?"* she mouthed, puzzled.

"As in climax."

Tory's face flamed. *"They're listening!"*

Marc smiled and touched the side of her swollen jaw. *"That's the general idea, princess. Scream your head off as if you are having the time of your life. Now."*

Tory produced a mangled scream. Marc's credible shout bounced off the walls. Still clutching her bare midriff, Tory shivered.

Marc pulled her half-naked body close and wrapped his arms around her. *"Good girl."*

He let her go and padded silently to the bedside table, picking up both glasses. He came back to her side and pressed a glass into her hand. Tory gulped down the wine until she felt its warmth stealing into her bloodstream. *"Now what?"*

"Now we take a shower." Marc's voice was thick as he took the glass out of her hand and set in on a nearby table.

"A sho-shower?"

She followed him into the bathroom and waited mutely as he closed the door, turned on the hard stream of water and started stripping off his clothes.

He unsnapped the front closure of her bra and tossed it on the floor. Her panties and stockings followed. Tory felt hypnotized as he tucked a hand towel around her cast and pushed her unresisting naked body under the warm spray.

"Now we can talk." He said with satisfaction as water sluiced down his face and over his broad shoulders. Tory felt the water plaster her hair to her skin. She

stared blankly at Marc's hairy chest. How on earth could he switch on and off like this?

She gave a muffled, choked sob and tried to open the clear glass door. Marc pulled her back against his chest. Turning her in his arms he said huskily, "You were terrific, princess."

Tears filled her eyes and she bit her lip. "I was petrified."

Marc's lips lowered to sip the water off her cheek. "This one is for us." His mouth slanted across hers and Tory choked back a sob as the sweet insistent pressure of his mouth opened hers.

The wet heat of his tongue and the familiar roughness of his chest sliding against her wet, naked breasts made her forget everything else. Desire flared in her, and her heart beat erratically as her nipples pressed against the familiar roughness and the hard muscles of his chest.

"Mmm." She couldn't get enough of him as she stood on tiptoe, her fingers clutched in his wet hair. His mouth ravished hers—too slowly, and she pressed her breasts flat against him, straining to get closer.

Her skin felt ultrasensitive as his hand traveled down her body, testing the shape of her nipples, the curve of her waist, the flair of her hips. He pressed her against the cool marble wall.

She slid her hand up the slick skin of his rib cage, tangling her fingers in the crisp damp hair on his chest. He smelled delicious and she darted her tongue out to taste him. She felt his flat nipple peak against the tip of her tongue and heard his groan of pleasure.

"The bed . . . ?" she asked hopefully.

"We'd never make it." He nibbled at the tendons in her neck. "Besides—" he sucked her skin into his mouth, laving it with his tongue "—the first time we make love in a bed, it *won't* be with God-only-knows-who listening in!" His breath fanned her neck deliciously. "God, I want you."

"You have me." Her body burned, yearning for his until she was almost incoherent. She felt the compelling pressure of his large hands cupping her hips, pulling her more tightly against his erection.

Tory managed to hook one leg behind his, pressing him closer, to the aching juncture of her thighs, then rotating her hips until he moved his hands to grip her buttocks.

As he lifted her, pinning her against the wall, she wrapped her legs around his waist. With one thrust, he entered the willing, wet, warmth of her. Tory moaned low in her throat as his thrusts became more intense, the in-out movement of his hips sliding her between the cool marble wall and the blazing heat of his body.

She closed her eyes as the heat and pressure built. Marc rubbed his coarse black chest hairs against her nipples, drawing a tortured whimper from Tory. She tried to press her hips closer, but Marc slowed his thrusts until he was barely moving.

"Slowly, sweetheart, slowly. I want this to last."

Tory was beyond waiting. She used her heels to clutch his bottom and pulled with all her strength, undulating her hips until his body movements matched hers.

At last the unbearable waves of pleasure crested. With a cry, she climaxed. An instant later, he followed.

Water sluicing steadily against his back, Marc slowly lowered her to her feet and pushed soaking strands of her hair over her shoulder. His arm came around her waist as he soaped her and helped her rinse. Dizzy, she leaned her head against his chest while he washed himself.

Her knees felt weak, and her heart pounded, yet she couldn't meet his eyes as he helped her out of the shower and handed her a towel.

Steam filled the bathroom as the shower roared behind the closed glass door. Marc took the towel out of her hand and quickly rubbed her dry. He slipped his finger under her chin. "You okay?"

"Yes." But she knew she would never be okay again. Today had shown her just how very different they were. She would never in a million wishful years, be able to fit into his life. He certainly wouldn't fit into hers.

She was scared out of her mind, at the same time as being sexually aware of him all the time. A mere glance made her want him. She loved the touch of his hands and mouth. She loved the way he enjoyed playing with her hair. She loved the way his pale eyes ignited when he touched her.

She loved. And that was the problem.

Marc Savin was hazardous to her health.

"When can we leave?" Tory asked, keeping her voice low under the sound of the water and wrapping the towel around her.

Marc ran his towel over his hair, using his hands to pull it back and tie it.

"I have to get Lynx out and to the chopper." He pulled on his pants and picked up his shirt from the floor. Ignoring the water marks on it, he shrugged it over his shoulders and started buttoning the studs. "Remember? I had you tell him I'd come down in two hours."

He took his watch out of his pocket, strapping it to his wrist. "That gives me about forty minutes to get you organized."

"I'm always organized," Tory said, sitting on the edge of the tub. "What do you want me to do?"

Marc pulled on his jacket and looked down at her. "I'm going to have to leave you here until he's safely away."

"No!" Tory shot up and clutched his arm. "No, Marc, you can't leave me here. I'll come with you. I'll help you with Alex...."

"Tory—" his voice was gentle "—you told me yourself that he's badly hurt. I can't watch out for both of you. I'll end up getting us all killed. I'll be back to get you, I promise." He rubbed his jaw. "If there was any other way, I'd take it. I hate like hell to leave you with those animals for even five minutes," he said, his voice grim. "But there is no other way."

She'd have to make do with that. She knew that it was the sensible, practical thing. But she was terrified of being here alone with those two men.

She waited until Marc, in Sir Ian's voice, thanked her ironically for a delightful evening. When the door had closed behind him she threw herself down on the bed and sobbed. She didn't care who was listening.

TORY WOKE TO SUNLIGHT streaming through the window. The wet towel lay beside her, and her hair, still damp, tangled around her naked body.

Aching all over, she dragged herself into the bathroom like an old woman. Her body hurt in a million places as she turned on the shower. The water revived her a little, and she sensed that Alex was gone.

Dressing in the clothes she'd selected the night before, she forced herself to dry her hair and tie it back with a silk scarf she found in a drawer. The black linen slacks were a little loose, and tucking in the white silk shirt, Tory went in search of a belt, cinching it around her waist. Tears stung her eyes and she bit her lip hard.

She didn't bother with makeup, and her heart was back up in her throat as she moved restlessly about the room.

Marc was gone. But he would come back and she had to pull herself together before he did. She almost jumped a foot when the door opened and she turned to see the malevolent gaze of Mario. He was carrying a cloth-covered tray.

"Breakfast? Good, I'm starving." The very thought of food made her sick to her stomach, but she knew she should appear as normal as possible. She thought she was fine until she saw who was standing behind Mario. *Oh, God.*

Ragno stepped aside and allowed Samuel Hoag to precede him into the room. He nodded at Mario to set down the tray, close the door and wait outside. "You've been a naughty girl, Miss Jones." Ragno's malicious voice would live forever in her nightmares. Tory felt bone-deep cold and the small hairs on her arms prickled as he moved closer. He was wearing an overpoweringly sweet and cloying after-shave.

Tory tilted her chin and straightened her back. "How is that?" *Stay calm*, she told herself. *Just stay calm. Marc will come—*

"I mentioned your little tryst with Sir Ian to my other guest last night." Ragno shook his head, his pink scalp shiny under his hair. "He was not pleased."

Tory raised her eyebrows. "Really?"

"No." Ragno's sausagelike fingers tightened on the silver-headed cane he held in his right hand. "In fact he was quite furious." Ragno circled the room, picking up a dusty perfume atomizer off the dressing table, lifting it to his nose and then putting it down.

Tory felt the end of the bed behind her knees. She glanced from Ragno, near the dressing table, back to Hoag at the door. "That doesn't surprise me, he's rather... possessive."

"Where is he, Miss Jones?" Ragno moved closer. She cringed inwardly as he stroked the icy metal head of the cane down her cheek. It burned.

"Where is who?"

The silver knob pressed against her cheekbone—hard. "Your former lover."

"I have absolutely no idea. He probably didn't like your hospitality any more than I have." The moment the angry words were out of her mouth, Tory knew she'd made a very bad mistake.

Cristoph Ragno tapped the cane harder on her cheek. It brought tears to her eyes. She bit the inside of her cheek, edging away.

Grabbing the hair tied at her nape, he said in a deadly voice, "We have two guards dead and another three wishing they were." He forced her head back and stared coldly into her terrified eyes. "Now, where are they, Miss Jones?"

Samuel Hoag had moved from the door and closer to the bed to block her retreat. She tried to pull Ragno's fingers from her hair. "I . . . I d-don't know."

Sweat glistened in the pink folds around Ragno's mouth. "We know both men are agents, Miss Jones. Not just any agents, but T-FLAC, to be precise. They have been messing in our business for years now. Poking their noses into things that are no concern of the United States. I am going to put a bloody end to the organization one way or another." His fingers clenched her hair close to her scalp in a stinging grip. "I'll start by cutting off T-FLAC's head. It has taken us five years to catch even one agent. The man we have held all these months couldn't be broken. Not so much as a name would he give us. If you hadn't arrived those weeks ago we would have had to kill him. But we knew you would be even better bait, Miss Jones. We had no idea just what your connection was, but Samuel was sure you would net us some results if we let you go and allowed you to run whimpering back to the States. And he was, as always, quite correct. All you have to do is tell us which one was the Phantom." Her mouth went dry. "Now, you can do this the easy way—" he twisted a wristful of hair and gave an excruciating tug "—or the hard way. I can assure you that either way will be satisfactory to me. Now I must admit that I'm the more— how shall I put this?—I'm the more physical of the two. But I can assure you that you will not enjoy Samuel's methods any more than you do mine. You are wearing my patience to a nub, Miss Jones. Speak, or forever hold your peace."

That was what she was afraid of. Tory licked dry lips. "I have no idea w-what you're talking a-about. I don't know anything about spies, for goodness' sake.... I honestly don't know what you mean."

This was her worst nightmare. She was paralyzed with terror as she realized that, unless Marc was hiding behind that closed door right now, she was on her own. Falling apart and crumpling into a whimpering little ball was not going to save her. To hell with it. Either way, she was going to have to get herself out of this mess.

"I *will* tell you this. If you don't let go of my hair right this damn minute I'm going to scream this pile of stone down and every government agent from every country on this planet will come and cut off *your* head! There are at least a dozen people who know exactly where I am and who I'm with. Now let me go!"

She screamed as he twisted her arm behind her back. He forced her arm higher, and the pain was exquisite.

Tory lashed out instinctively with her cast. The sound of it connecting with his face blocked out by her own shriek of agony as he twisted her hand impossibly higher against her back. A thin trickle of blood oozed from his nose where her cast had connected. *Oh, God! So much for taking a stand!*

"She must like pain." Ragno said mildly, taking out a crumpled handkerchief and dabbing at his nostril.

Ragno dropped her arm as suddenly as he'd grabbed it. It hung numbly at her side.

"I ask you one more time, Miss Jones. Where are they? And which one is the Phantom?"

Tory suspected they would give her only so much time to answer before they killed her. Either way, it wasn't going to be pleasant. "You keep asking me the same questions," Tory said, biting her lip. "The last time I saw S-Sir Ian was after dinner last night. He left me and I don't know where he went."

His arm lashed out and the cane whistled as it came down across her back. Tory screamed.

She saw the arm swing back again. It was stopped in midflight by Samuel Hoag's bony hand.

"I think Miss Jones has had enough, my friend. There are other ways . . ." Hoag said grimly, looking at Victoria. "Aren't there, my dear?"

Tory gauged the distance to the door. With almost superhuman strength, her gasping breath almost choking her, she broke free from the two men and ran for the door. The handle slipped out of her sweaty grasp as she felt a hand on the back of her shirt and she was pulled off-balance.

"No!" Using her legs, she kicked out at Hoag as he plucked her away from the door and dragged her back into the center of the room. With a brutal shove to her chest, he pushed her down on the bed.

Before she could even bounce, she was scrambling backward, coming against the ornate satin headboard. "Don't come near me."

She could tell by the murderous rage in Ragno's face that it was a pathetic command. Hoag held him back as he tried to beat her with the silver-headed cane. The sound of the cane thumping the satin spread filled the room. Dust hung in the sunlit air. Tory stared at the glinting silver head as it came closer and closer. Her mouth dry, she pressed her spine into the soft fabric at her back, twisting her legs out of reach. It was a total waste of time, of course.

Marc, where are you? she thought frantically as Hoag went to the door and spoke to Mario outside. Closing the door, he jerked his head for Ragno to get out of the way and seated himself at the foot of the bed. Tory, now on her knees, scooted farther back, trying to make herself a smaller target.

"My friend is a little zealous in his quest for the truth, Miss Jones." His voice was deep and devoid of expression. Tory tried to stop shaking, and she fixed her gaze on his face.

Behind him, Ragno impatiently tapped the cane on the carpet. Its thumping sounds syncopated with the thump of her heart. "There are ways to make even a whore like you talk, and I assure you we will use every one of them until you do." He turned his head as Mario came back into the room, followed by Giorgio.

Hoag motioned to the two men. "Hold her."

Almost catatonic with fear, Tory glanced from one side of the bed to the other. She had no idea what they were planning, but she knew it would be bad. Very bad.

She bucked and kicked with all her strength, but they managed to catch her flailing arms and legs and spread-eagled her flat on the bed.

Hoag lifted the small box Mario had brought in on the tray, extracting a hypodermic needle. Tory stared with morbid fascination as he plunged the end and a thin stream of liquid spurted from the sharp tip.

Her back arched frantically off the bed as he came toward her. The needle sparkled in the sunlight coming through the window.

She licked her parched lips. "Please. Oh please . . ." Her eyes went wild as he pushed up the sleeve of her shirt.

"A little phenobarbital, Miss Jones. It won't hurt a bit." She felt the first sharp prick of the needle under her skin then a rush of heat surged through her veins. Her vision clouded and her lids closed. Just before everything went black she heard Ragno say in a sibilant hiss, "You gave her too much, goddamn it, Samuel. You gave her too—"

MARC FELT FOR the pulse at the base of her throat with fingers he had to force to remain steady. It was pitch-dark, but he hadn't dared turn on the flashlight. Her pulse was weak but stable.

"Thank God." He shook her by the shoulders, and when she moaned, he pressed his hand across her mouth.

"Victoria." Urgency made his voice as cutting as a knife. "You've got to wake up! Do you hear me?"

She didn't move. He shook her again. Harder this time, beginning to realize this was no ordinary sleep. They had ten minutes—fifteen, tops—before someone found the unconscious guards down the hall.

He pulled her upper body against his chest, her head flopped to his shoulder. Shit, he couldn't carry her and hope to protect her—and he wouldn't leave her, either. Thank God they'd brought her down to the dungeon. He'd managed to find her after an hour of searching upstairs and then only with the unwilling cooperation of one of Ragno's men. But this location sure as hell beat hauling her from one end of the immense castle to the other to get out.

From here, it was a fairly straight route—up the back stairs and into the front hall. If he could get her to wake up, they might just make it. He wanted like hell to hold her and he needed to see her in the light to assure himself she was all right. He had time for neither.

"Damn it, Victoria, do you hear me?" he demanded fiercely, pushing her head off his shoulder and holding it in both hands. "If you don't wake up and move your ass, we're dead meat!"

He felt her stir, and he slapped her face. Her head moved to the side slowly, and she whimpered, trying to pull away.

"Marc?" Her voice was weak, but at least she was conscious.

"Come on, Tory!" He hauled her to her feet and waited a second while she got her balance. "Up and at 'em, princess." She wilted against him. Marc forced her to walk from one side of the small cell to the other and then back again, keeping his ears tuned to any noises outside.

By the time he'd walked her back and forth a dozen times, her gait was steadier.

"Do you know what they gave you?" he asked urgently as he eased his supporting arm away to see if she was capable of standing on her own.

"Pheno—something."

"Barbital." He felt her falter, but kept his hands off her. If she was going to make it out of here alive, she was going to have to do it on her own two feet. "How long ago?" His voice was harsh in the darkness.

"This morning sometime."

"Good. It should be pretty much out of your system by now. Keep walking," he barked, as her steps lagged. He heard the shuffle of her feet on the stone as he went back to the cot and tossed a canvas bag on the stinking mattress.

"Ever used a gun?"

"No."

"Well, there's always a first time. Come over here."

When she got close enough, he took her hand and wrapped her fingers around the laser-sighted automatic. He tightened his fingers over hers when she tried to jerk her hand away. "Listen and listen good, princess. Both our lives depend on you getting yourself pulled together. Now, concentrate while I tell you how to use this."

After he was sure she understood the basics, he pulled her behind him and checked the corridor. Everything was quiet.

Keeping Tory at his back, Marc walked carefully toward the stairs. If anyone came now, they would be in one hell of a bind. There was nowhere to go. The wall sconces, spaced every twenty feet, cast dim amber light the length of the corridor. There were far too many shadows and recessed doorways for comfort.

He glanced at Victoria out of the corner of his eye. Her face was stark white, and her eyes dark and terrified, but she was on her feet and moving. The automatic hung from her hand—away from her body as if she felt the damn thing would bite. He used his own weapon to tilt the infrared up. "Keep it there," he said harshly. She nodded, gripping the gun more firmly between both hands. The dammed cast interfered with the balance, but at least it looked as if it was at a useable angle.

The stairs ahead were curved and dangerous, and he motioned for her to stay directly behind him as he climbed steadily. If anybody decided to come down, they would be at a distinct disadvantage.

He breathed a sigh of relief when he saw the light at the top.

Still moving silently, he motioned for her to follow him as he kept to the wall, heading for the sitting room where he'd first seen her last night.

At last reaching the double doors, he opened one and motioned her in behind him, then closed it silently. The room was empty and quiet as he moved to the door at the other end.

He cursed. The palace was enormous, with doors everywhere and a million places to hide. Unfortunately that meant there were hiding places for the bad guys, too. The only way out was through the main foyer and out the front door— If they were lucky enough to pass through undetected. He'd disabled the motion detector when he'd come in for Lynx, but that didn't mean that there wasn't some conscientious guard out there, just waiting for them.

He thought of Lynx in the chopper, waiting for them like a sitting duck. How the son of a bitch thought he could fly in the condition he was in was beyond him. But he wasn't leaving without his sister.

Marc could understand the sentiment.

He glanced over his shoulder at Victoria. The silk Paisley scarf tying back her hair had slipped, loosening the long strands, and her eyes were wide with fright.

His gut tightened at the smudged tearstains on her pale cheeks. When she moved the snout of the gun up a notch and tilted her chin, he almost smiled. Bowed but not beaten. Damn, what a woman.

Admiration swelled his chest. He briefly touched the red mark on her cheek. "Let's go."

It was one in the morning, the household was asleep and the foyer was blessedly empty. He heard the squeak of Victoria's shoes behind him on the slick marble as his eyes scanned the wide-open expanse. The heavy front doors were about forty yards ahead of them. Beyond that was the drawbridge and then the formal gardens and freedom.

Marc indicated that they were going to take a chance on cutting a diagonal across to the door. It was a calculated risk. Keeping to the walls would give them more cover but would also take longer, and time was of the essence.

Victoria nodded and got ready to run. Her magnificent hair trailed down her back, one sleeve of her white shirt was still pushed up, and Marc could see the bruise made by the needle. He forgot the red haze of fury that threatened to blind him. He was going to enjoy like hell coming back to beat the crap out of those bastards. But first things first. Gritting his teeth, Marc scanned the foyer one last time. Grabbing Tory's elbow, he sprinted across the slippery marble tile. He felt her skid and paused briefly to steady her, then dragged her close behind him again. She was breathing hard and he felt the heat emanating from her body as she pressed close.

They reached the door and his hands quickly slipped its bolts. They groaned and rattled, but the door opened. After a quick reconnoiter he went through first.

In front of them was an immense courtyard. Marc held her back with his arm as he scanned the shadowy open ground between them and the gate in the far wall.

In the center was an enormous three-tiered fountain. There was no water spouting from it, and the moonlight glistened off the green moss and slime in the basins.

High walls surrounded them on three sides; the dark windows of the castle were at their backs. The walls made good, deep shadows and he took her arm, putting her past the shrubbery along the side of the castle, keeping in shadow.

She followed him closely, stopping when he stopped, keeping the same distance between them. He breathed easier when they had traversed the unprotected space between the castle and the surrounding wall. His feet flattened the tall weeds, making a path through the overgrown garden beside the wall. They were almost there.

He dared not take the chance that someone might be looking out the window and would take a potshot. Victoria followed him, silent except for her ragged breathing. He looked back to make sure she was still upright.

Her face was deathly pale and streaked with dirt, with strands of hair plastered to her sweat-dampened skin. Marc cursed silently and nodded toward the pedestrian gate beside the tall portcullis that led outside.

She nodded, lifting the gun in her hands higher. They came to the small door in the wall that he'd left unlocked when he'd come in. "Almost there," he said under his breath, pushing it open and pulling her through behind him. It was too good to be true. Were Spider's men all so incompetent they hadn't noticed that she was missing? Marc glanced at his watch in the moonlight, surprised that it had taken them only sixteen minutes to get from the dungeon to outside the walls.

The medieval drawbridge spanned the moat, which was more mud than water. Urging her to move faster, Marc sped across the warped wood timbers and toward the gardens and the cover of the trees.

He could smell the rotten stink of stagnant water and heard Victoria's breath, as she panted behind him, his feet biting into the gravel of the driveway. They would be clear targets, out here in the open. But there was no alternative; they had to make a run for it.

"Tory, listen to me. We have to run hard for those trees over there. If you hear anything—anything at all—ignore it and run faster. I'll be right behind you."

"Okay." In the moonlight, her eyes were wide terrified pools.

Marc looked at the heavy gun clutched in her arms. He considered losing it so that she could run faster. But the fact was, whether she really had to use it or not, if something happened to him, she would at least have a chance of protecting herself. He pushed the laser gun more firmly into her grasp. "Remember how to use it?"

She nodded, "Red light, shoot."

"Let's go."

The moon, unfortunately, was almost full and it was as bright as daylight. Victoria's white shirt was a perfect target as they ran hell-for-leather toward the trees, the crunch of the small stones under their feet sounding dangerously loud. As soon as they were under cover he would give her his shirt. But first they had to get there.

The gravel driveway circling the moat was a wide, pale, unprotected swath they had to cross before they could even get to the shrub-studded lawn and the small forest that rimmed the estate.

Their feet hit grass as they sprinted for the thick cover of the trees. A high-pitched whine warned Marc a second too late that they hadn't been so lucky, after all. The force of the bullet slicing his forehead, dropped him to one knee. The pain would come later. He ignored it.

Staggering to his feet, he felt the warmth of blood running into his eyes. Victoria had stopped dead, her white shirt blinding in the moonlight.

"Run like hell, damn it!" Marc shouted.

8

THE SOUND OF RUNNING feet across the gravel behind him warned Marc that the bad guys were hot on their trail. There was another ping as a bullet whizzed by and tore up the grass between them. "Get the hell out of here!" he was yelling at her, as he felt the air part from another bullet.

Glancing over his shoulder, he saw a flash of light, and seconds later heard a blast of fire from the drawbridge. Somehow he managed to gather Victoria in one arm, and twisted to spray the area behind them with a violent burst from the Uzi.

The outline of a man reeling over the drawbridge, and the satisfying splash as a body hit the water was drowned out as another round of bullets ricocheted close to their feet. Grass and dirt sprayed as Marc pushed her forward, his arm propelling her as he returned fire. "Go, for Christ's sake!" He hauled her up as she stumbled in the soft dirt, and pushed her hard.

"I'm not leaving without you."

The fool woman turned back and waited for him as Marc staggered toward her, blood dripping down into his eye. He caught at her cast and hauled her as fast as he could go. A hundred yards, eighty yards, fifty yards.

The manicured lawn took a beating, sod flying as bullets whizzed too close for comfort. He almost tripped over a boxwood hedge but kept pushing and pulling at Victoria to keep her abreast.

The trees swayed slightly in the breeze, their dark branches beckoning when he felt a sting in his leg. Then, twenty yards from cover the leg folded under him and he fell to the ground.

Damn. The sons of bitches were in front as well as behind them. The blood dripping down his face reminded him that these bastards weren't playing. Pointing the Uzi at a burst of light, he fired off several rounds. There was a scream and a thud as someone bit the dust.

The Uzi was good for another sixty-four rounds times three, with the second magazine welded to the first, but at the rate the bad guys were going, he would be out of ammo long before they were.

He shot another round into the trees ahead of him. It bought Victoria precious seconds as the shooting stopped for a moment.

He pulled himself painfully to his feet. He was going to get them both killed if he couldn't get Victoria the hell and away.

All he could see of her was that damned white shirt through the branches, and as he did a staggering run, he tugged the black T-shirt over his head. The night air felt good as it cooled the sweat on his body. His leg burned like fire.

He threw her the shirt, pulling her down behind the cover of the shrubs. The heavy scent of gardenias permeated the air.

"Put it on, and do it fast." His breath was a choppy whisper. He could hear the goons thrashing about in the trees. It was mercifully darker, the tall trees and thick ornamental shrubs hiding them. But for how long?

Victoria pulled the shirt over her head and then leaned close, "You're hurt!" Her cool hand moved over his face, as if she could fix him with her fingertips. "Marc! You're bleeding!"

"Yeah, bullets have a tendency to do that." He dug in his pocket and then grabbed her wrist as she tried to use the hem of the shirt to stanch the flow. "Here's the ignition key to a Vespa parked off the main road up there. I want you to move carefully that way." With his head he indicated the direction through the trees. "The moped is behind the barn. Drive it to where I picked you up in the truck, and get yourself to the grotto. They've blocked the way. There's no way we can get to the helicopter now. Alex is waiting for my signal. He'll pick you up."

"I'm not leaving without you!"

"You'll damn well do as I tell you! Move your butt out of here. Now!" The crashing of small branches drowned out his whispered words as men ran within feet of their hiding place. Marc put his hand over her mouth as she started to speak.

But she shook her head, her eyes were huge over his hand. She wasn't leaving without him.

When the noise moved away, he dropped his hand and said furiously, "You're no goddamned hero. You'll get me killed if you stick around."

He saw her flinch at the contempt in his words, but she just said flatly, "Then we go together. I'm not leaving without you!"

Marc thought quickly and put a sneer in his voice. "Just because I screwed you doesn't give you the right to hang around like a frigging leech. Have some pride, Victoria. I only wanted your body, not a lifetime commitment." He heard the sharp hiss of her breath and pushed harder. "At least Krista would have been some help."

He wished she wouldn't look at him like that and squinted off into the trees. "When I want a woman, it sure as hell wouldn't be some mousy little bookkeeper from the sticks." He looked her straight in the eye. "Get lost, lady. Your brother's waiting for you and I have things to do."

Ignoring the way her eyes narrowed and her chin tilted, Marc moved away from her, crawling deeper into the trees without a backward glance. In moments he was swallowed by the dense underbrush. He continued as fast as his leg allowed until he was sure he was far enough away from her. He leaned back, using a tree trunk to rest his leg for a moment, hoping to God she could figure out where the hell the Vespa was.

Marc knew the only way to draw their fire was for them to find him first. He crashed through the undergrowth, making enough noise for a deaf man to follow. He didn't have long to wait.

Mario came around a tree trunk, his eyes darting from side to side, an AK-47 assault rifle cradled in his arms like a baby. Marc took advantage of the man's surprise seeing him just standing there in the glade. Marc swung his leg up in an arc. The side of his foot hit the rifle, sending it somersaulting into the bushes.

Mario's hands were now free, and he managed to get a glancing blow to Marc's face, but Marc sidestepped, bringing the butt of his Uzi up and ramming it against the other man's cheek. Mario screamed in pain, his eyes feral as he swung again.

The blow landed on Marc's forehead, exactly where the bullet had creased him. Damn. Marc exploded, blocking the other man's blows and striking out in a flurry—left elbow to the throat, right fist to the gut. He swung his leg again, but the bullet wound made his arc too low and he hit Mario's shoulder this time.

Mario staggered back, blood pouring from his nose. He looked around frantically for help. There was none. Marc gave him a shove with the butt of the Uzi.

"How do you like feeling helpless, you little piece of crap?" Marc punched him in the solar plexus. "This is for touching my woman." He swung again, knocking the other man's head to the side.

Finally he dropped Mario with a vicious uppercut to his jaw. The sound of bone crunching was extremely satisfying. Mario lay still, and Marc used the back of his free hand to wipe the blood out of his eyes. He was starting to feel a whole lot better. His adrenaline was pumping, he didn't even feel the blood on his face, and his leg was numb. One down and—

"Drop your weapon, Sir Ian. Or should I say Phantom?"

Marc obediently dropped the Uzi as Ragno emerged from the tree, flanked by Giorgio and another man. Ragno held a .45 Magnum semiautomatic—no match for the Uzi, but that was flat on the ground at his feet. Ragno's two goons held AK-47 assault rifles pointed at his chest.

He figured that Victoria needed another ten minutes to get away. He shifted his weight off his bad leg and waited, looking deceptively relaxed. When Ragno yelled for the rest of the men, Marc relaxed even more. Right now, all he could do was stall.

"You have proved a great inconvenience to my operation for many years," Ragno said coldly, the tips of his jutting ears were pink, and his uniform of U.S. Army fatigues looked ridiculously out of place on his bulky frame. "I should shoot you where you stand."

Marc shrugged. "It would seem expedient."

"You are very cocky for a man who might well bleed to death," Ragno continued coldly. "Move over there." He indicated a stout tree. Marc dragged his game leg more than it warranted and shuffled to the tree.

"Tie him up." Ragno pulled a cloth out of his breast pocket and swiped it down his face as he watched his men dispassionately. "Test those bonds to make sure he can't get loose."

Two men, using thin wire, bound his hands and feet and stood at attention on either side of him. Marc leaned back against the knotty bark and tested the strength of his bonds. Tight and efficient. He sighed.

"Before I kill you slowly, Phantom, I want to know how many of your operatives know of my whereabouts." Ragno moved closer now that Marc was tied, still flanked by his small army.

"Operatives?" Marc mocked. "I don't know what you mean, old chap."

At a nod from Ragno, a fist landed on Marc's cheekbone, snapping his head back. Pain sliced through him and his stomach heaved as a series of blows landed— on the ribs a couple of times, then the face, the kidneys. Yeah, the guy was definitely a pro.

"What happened to your pal, Tweedle-Dee?" Marc managed.

"Shut up! I will ask the questions."

"Go right ahead. I'm a little tied up right now, but I certainly have the time."

Ragno's eyes blazed. "You insolent fool. Answer my questions." He nodded to the guard on Marc's left. The man used his full strength to punch him in the solar plexus. Nothing like a fair division of labor. Marc's breath whooshed out of his lungs and he slumped back against the tree.

"I like games, Phantom. Very much." Ragno's breath stank as he pushed his face close to Marc's. "But I much prefer to play by my own rules. We enjoyed a little game with your slut this morning." He stroked the side of his perspiring face with his handkerchief and smiled. "She's quite feisty, isn't she?" A nod of his head and the guard on his right punched Marc again. "She will screw anyone."

With effort, Marc kept his expression bland. Ragno tried a different tack. "How many of your people know of our whereabouts?"

"Let's just say that enough people know who and what you are to effectively eliminate you and your entire little merry band." Marc managed to press his body upright against the tree, as he looked at Ragno contemptuously. "You don't for a moment think that I came in alone, do you?"

"We will find them and eliminate every one."

"You and what army?" Marc sneered, blinking into the flashlights trained on his face. Where the hell was Victoria? He strained to hear the putt-putt of the moped. Other than the wind ruffling the treetops and Ragno's uneven breathing, the forest was silent.

Ragno stepped closer still, and Marc wrinkled his nose at his stench. Christ, did this ass never take a bath? "I have an army," Ragno said smugly, fingering the collar of his fatigues.

"Yeah, the Salvation Army. Get real. What are you going to do? Talk us to death?"

Ragno snapped Marc's head back with an open-handed blow.

HIDDEN IN THE TREES, Tory winced. All she could see was the back of Marc's head as it slammed to the side. But she could see Cristoph Ragno's face and torso quite clearly.

Sweat stung her eyes and she used her shoulder to blot her face. The sound of the men's voices was almost obliterated by the thundering of her heart. Her hands, around the gun, felt slick and shaky. Oh, God, could she do it?

Not giving herself time to think, she edged closer. Something snapped under her left foot and she froze, her heart in her mouth. No one seemed to notice. She was as close as she dared. If she reached out her arm she could have touched Marc's shoulder. The gun suddenly seemed to weigh a ton. What did she know about guns, for heaven's sake? What if she shot Marc by mistake? The what ifs buzzed in her head—but for only a second. Krista would have done it without blinking an eye.

Very carefully Tory eased the gun firmly into her left hand using the cast for balance, she turned on the laser and aimed. A red dot, the size of a dime wavered on Ragno's shoulder. Then crawled, very, very slowly. Across his chest, his collar, his throat, and then paused. Tory held her breath trying to steady the beam. She'd forgotten how to breath. How could the man not feel the heat of that red light? Tory moved the red beam unsteadily up the sweat glistening on Ragno's neck, up and up until it was aligned between his close set eyes. For a moment she hesitated.... She squeezed the trigger.

A second later she heard the pop. Then there was pandemonium. She refused to look, as she ran from behind the cover of the trees, brandishing her gun.

She heard Marc's, "Hot damn!" but couldn't look at him. Suddenly calm, she lifted the weapon in steady hands and did a slow arc with the barrel.

Marc rubbed his face on his shoulder as Victoria came through the trees. The men stood stupefied, watching the small woman with the gun step into the clearing. Her hair swung wildly around her, the sleeves of the white silk blouse stuck out below the short sleeves of his black T-shirt, and there was a rip in the knee of her black slacks. She looked magnificent. She looked furious.

"Drop your weapons," Tory snapped, eyeing the men warily, the nose of the infrared moving from one to the other. They obeyed.

She nodded to the man closest to Marc. "Untie him."

As he felt the wire loosen, Marc brought his hands in front of him, rubbing his wrists. The man bent to free his feet. As soon as the bonds were loose, Marc kicked out with his good leg. The man flipped to the side and lay still on the ground.

Victoria hadn't turned the weapon off, and the red dot made a small target on the man's chest.

"He's unconscious, green eyes. Don't worry about this one."

Marc caught a movement out of the corner of his eye as someone tried to get up. "Victoria! Left!"

She raised the gun and pinned the other man in place. He dropped the pistol.

"Hurry up!" Victoria's voice rose. Marc could see the fine tremor in her hands and hoped that the men couldn't. He stepped over the unconscious man, his game leg numb, but he sure as hell wasn't going to wait around for Victoria to be rushed by seven men. Limping, he came quickly to her side and took the gun from her hands.

All seven men backed up. "Over there." Marc used the gun to indicate their dead leader and they reluctantly bunched around him.

"Strip," he ordered.

They looked at him blankly.

"Get naked, gentlemen, and don't mind the lady." Over his shoulder he said grimly, "Find the Uzi—I dropped it back over there." He wished his damned leg had stayed numb. He could feel warm blood pulsing out of the wound.

She came back as the last man peeled off his underwear. She averted her eyes as Marc said, "Drop." They all fell in the dirt, facedown. "Grab their belts and whatever else you can find and start tying them up." Marc knew he needed to get her moving so she wouldn't have time to think about what she'd just done.

He could see that she was in shock, but she did as he said, stripping belts from loops and shoelaces out of their shoes. He gave her top marks as she tied their hands and feet so that their legs were bent up at an unnatural angle, pointing at their heads.

"Good girl, you're doing fine." He was going to pass out soon and he resisted with everything in him. She'd come this far. He needed at least to see her safely to the grotto.

He gave the seven trussed-up men one more glance, assessing their chances of breaking free, and took Victoria's arm to get her away.

After several yards he knew that there was no way that he was going to walk out of there on his own two feet. He'd lost too much blood, his vision was next to useless, and his leg wouldn't support his weight. He stopped to lean against a tree. "Princess, you have to get to the grotto and meet up with Lynx. Tell him where I am and he'll send someone back for me when you're safe."

She didn't bother answering him; she just pushed her shoulder under his arm and held tightly to his hand dangling between her breasts, forcing him to walk. The forest wasn't thick; it was more ornamental than wild. But still the going was rough. Thick shrubbery had grown between the trees, and the pathways were obliterated by the debris of fallen leaves and branches.

It could have been hours but it was probably no more than forty minutes when Victoria slowed her pace. They had come to the road.

They were both breathing hard, and Marc was tortured by the fact that she'd practically carried him all this way. He could feel the sweat making her clothes stick to her slender back.

Tory's breathing was labored as she spoke—"I'll g-get—the Ves-pa." She moved from under his arm and steadied him against the side of a rusted tractor that had been abandoned at the side of the road. "I'll be right back."

"Victoria . . ." But she didn't have time to listen to what he had to say. Every muscle in her body burned, she didn't want to pause long enough to think. If she paused for even a second, now, she would be lost. Her legs pumped faster as she rounded the barn and saw the scooter, partially hidden.

Marc tossed his good leg over the back of the seat as Victoria pulled up. "Go!" he said tersely, settling his hands in front of her to grip the pommel.

She went. The moped didn't go more than thirty-five miles an hour, but they were moving in the right direction and hopefully had enough leeway for a clean getaway.

Tory's hair whipped in her face as she angled her body roughly to take a curve. This was suicide and she knew it. She was riding the unsteady scooter with a total disregard for their safety. The rearview mirror showed no headlights. But that could be as temporary as the next curve.

"Keep it steady," Marc warned against her cheek. His head felt like a log as he rested his chin on her shoulder.

The wind stung her cheeks and made her eyes water, but she concentrated on keeping them upright. The noise of the little moped was so loud. She wanted to look behind to see if they were being followed, but she didn't dare.

It was almost as bright as daylight as they rounded the outside wall of Pavina, heading toward the beach and the grotto. The narrow wheels slithered on the cobblestones before hitting the tarred road.

The Vespa was unpredictable on rough roads and gravel. The last time Tory had attempted to ride one was on her first visit to Marezzo. That time she'd traveled at a sedate ten miles an hour, ignoring the impa-

tient drivers that honked their horns at her. This time
she pushed the little moped as fast as it would go.

She felt Marc's body slump, and she was terrified he
would fall off. She almost cried with relief when his
arms tightened around her, and she took the dirt road
toward the cliffs in a spray of gravel and dust.

The moped stopped in a shower of sand just as she
felt his body slipping to the side. She managed to swing
her arm back, supporting him while she kicked down
the stand.

Using her body to prop him up she managed to swing
her legs off the Vespa and looked down at him, biting
her lip.

"Marc! Marc, up and at 'em. We have to get into the
grotto so you can call Alex. Marc?" His head lolled on
her chest. She pushed at him. "Marc, please. You have
to wake up."

Glancing nervously over her shoulder, she saw the
lights of a car coming down the main road toward
them. Then she looked at the beach. The tide was out,
the sand glistening in the moonlight was damp and hard
packed, and the ocean was bright.

Tory scanned the horizon for the helicopter and Alex.
The sky was empty. She bit her lip. Was she supposed
to wait on the beach? Or had Marc and Alex devised
some brilliant escape that they had forgotten to share
with her?

"Marc, wake up!"

His eyes opened blearily as he stared up at her and
then shook his head. "Lost too m-much blood. Go!"

"Oh, shut up!" Tory bit her lip. They moved slowly down the beach, her arms under his as she steered an erratic path down the hard-packed sand.

She had to take the risk of being spotted by staying close to the waterline where the sand was hardest. Nearer the cliff it was fine and dry and littered with rocks.

Her arms ached, as did her jaw from gritting her teeth, but they finally made it to the base of the grotto. Looking over her shoulder she saw the waves had washed out the tire tracks. Now all she had to do was get Marc up a mountain of rocks and rubble to the top. It was only thirty feet or so. She could do it. She *had* to.

It wasn't quite as bad as she'd expected. He was conscious enough to help, although sometimes it took a pinch or harsh words to get him moving. It was slow and torturous but they finally dragged themselves into the mouth of the cave.

Sprawled flat beside Marc, Tory struggled to draw breath into her heaving lungs. Sweat stung her eyes, but she didn't have time for that now.

She sat up and shook him. "Crawl over to where the bathrooms are," she instructed. He'd never make it back to camp and she didn't want to be trapped back there if they were found. "Do you hear me Marc? Crawl . . ."

"I hear you, General." Marc struggled to sit up, a lopsided grin brightening his white face. "You are one hell of a woman, you know that?"

"How do we get hold of Alex?"

"Done. I called him back there before I found you. If . . . we're not back at the chopper site, he'll look for us here." His voice faded and his eyes drooped. Victoria shoved him, hard.

"I'm awake." He didn't sound it, but his voice was strong enough for Victoria to know he wasn't going to pass out again for a while. "Got . . . to . . . get . . . bike . . . ." He licked his dry lips as he rested his head against the rock wall. In the moonlight his face was a sickly gray.

"What?"

"They'll . . . see it. Moon too . . . bright."

Victoria gave a silent groan. "I'll be right back."

The moped was on its side at the base of the rocks. Tory looked from it up the side of the cliff and down again, shaking her head. It had been all but impossible to push and prod Marc up that steep incline. How on earth was she going to pull the Vespa up there?

She looked around for a good hiding place, but there wasn't one. The rocks and boulders were large, but they were too close together. So she dragged the moped up and over the boulders, panting and swearing when she had the breath for it and mentally using all the cusswords she'd heard Marc use when she didn't.

She pulled it the last few feet and sank to the ground, her head on her knees. It would have been nice to take a rest, but unfortunately there wasn't time. Marc was back there and she needed to check the wound in his leg. God only knew what the next round held for them.

As she pushed the Vespa down the rocky corridor toward the lake, she prayed Alex would arrive with help soon. Marc had been right about one thing: she was no hero. Alex couldn't arrive soon enough.

Pushing faster, she wheeled it into the alcove that held the three Porta Potties and out of sight of the entrance.

Marc had propped himself against the far wall by the lake. "Lady, I have to say I'd have you on my side any day of the week." His voice sounded stronger but Victoria ignored the useless compliment. If being by his side required that she got shot at, she would pass, thank you very much.

"I'm going to get the first-aid kit. Is there anything else you need from camp?" She didn't like the gray color of his skin.

He closed his eyes at her militant tone and leaned his head back against the wall. "Bring the A.L.I.C.E. pack."

The camp was exactly as they had left it. Tory bundled both survival blankets into the pack and looked around to see if anything else could be useful. The matches lay beside the small propane stove, and she shoved them into her breast pocket and then picked up the heavy pack, slinging it over her shoulder.

Marc looked slightly better when she returned.

She wrinkled her nose as he chewed a couple of dry aspirin—the water bottle and cups were back at the camp. His leg was a mess; drying blood had stuck the pant leg to his skin.

"I think the bullet is still in here."

"Trust me. It's not." Marc's lips were white. "Just clean around it as best you . . . Shhhh!"

There was a scrape outside, as if a shoe had scuffed over stone. She and Marc froze, then Tory crawled silently to the opening into the main cavern. She glanced over her shoulder and raised four fingers. Four men.

Marc swore, tightening his belt around his thigh, and motioned for her to stay were she was. She watched the four men circle the lake, spreading out at the end to look for them.

When she turned back, Marc was hobbling to his feet and doing something on the side of the moped. For one hysterical moment she thought he was going to ride the blasted thing down the side of the cliff.

He pulled the gas cylinder out of the A.L.I.C.E. pack, holding it up triumphantly.

"What are you doing?" she whispered.

"We're going to pour this on the lake." He hefted the spare can and indicated the moped. "Roll that over to the water."

Tory moved the Vespa out of its hiding place, and crouched down as low as she could between the shrubs and ferns. She followed Marc to the edge of the lake.

Marc unscrewed the cap and carefully poured the gasoline into the water. When he was sure the container was empty, he tilted the moped and allowed the gasoline to drain from the tank.

"Get out of those pants and shoes," he whispered, his hand at his buttoned fly. "Leave on the T-shirt." His jeans dropped to the sandy floor a moment before hers did.

Marc's head disappeared around the edge of rock facing the lake. Seeing the back of his leg made bile rise in her throat. She avoided looking at the bruised and bloody discolored flesh. Crouching behind him, she settled her hand on his warm, bare shoulder.

One of the men had discovered their camp. He called to the others and they all disappeared behind the wall. Marc motioned her to move slowly behind him toward the lake.

His face glowed eerily in the diffused sapphire light of the water as he made room for her between the shrubs. The ground cover was cool and damp under her bare feet. Moisture from the fern dripped on her cheek and she brushed it off impatiently. She could feel the heat of Marc's leg pressed up against hers, and she tried to hold her breath for a moment to regulate it.

The four men came back around the rock wall, two on either side of the lake. Tory pressed closer to Marc. "Now what?"

Keeping his eyes straight ahead, Marc said softly, "Now we wait until they get to . . . oh, about to that little tree over there—

"Damn!" He patted his bare hip. "The matches are in the pack!"

Tory wordlessly dug into her breast pocket and slapped the matches onto Marc's bare knee.

He looked startled for a moment and then cupped her face. "You are one sweetheart of a partner. Stick by me, kid— I'll have you out of here in a flash." Dropping a quick kiss on her open mouth, he turned back to watch as the men got closer and closer.

"Why can't we just make a run for it?" Tory whispered desperately. She was getting a very bad feeling about this. The gasoline had spread in a thin oily film over the water. She rested her hand on Marc's arm. "We can slip by them, can't we?"

"We left the guns back there, Tory, and they'll see us as soon as we break cover. Beside, there are sure to be more of them waiting for us outside. We have to have a diversion." He paused. "Listen."

The chop-chop of the helicopter was unmistakable. All four men paused for a fraction of a second, then moved faster, flanking the lake and moving swiftly toward them and the only exit.

He handed her a small cylinder and showed her how to clamp the mouthpiece so that she could breathe underwater. "Get ready." Marc struck a match, flinging his arm up and over, he tossed it several yards out across the water. At the same time, he cried, "Jump!"

As they hit the water the flaming match ignited the gasoline. The sheet of fire spread rapidly, covering at least a third of the lake. Tory's head bobbed above the surface, her eyes wide as she saw the flames sweeping toward them. Marc, grabbing her arm, pulled her inexorably toward the whirlpool.

Eyes burning from the thick smoke, Tory trod water, feeling the pull of the whirlpool, then a steadying strength as Marc wrapped his arms tightly around her waist. She could hear the shouts of the men converging on the bank and then more running footsteps as they called for reinforcements.

Over the mouth mask she saw the flames at eye level coming closer and closer. She put both arms around Marc's waist, he kicked his feet until they were swept into the vortex of churning water. The fire was spreading, sweeping the gasoline toward them in a blazing sheet of orange and purple.

The voices got closer and louder. A gunshot reverberated against the cave walls, another splashed into the water close enough to spray her shoulder.

"Use the oxygen!" Marc inhaled deeply, his grip tightening. The sucking motion of the water caught her legs and pulled her under, and she squeezed her eyes shut as she held on tight.

For a split second she wondered how Marc was going to hold that breath for however long it took to get through the forty-foot tunnel and out to the open sea. Then she could think of nothing at all.

Their descent was swift. The smooth stone walls of the tunnel were the only thing holding them right side up, as the force of the water pulled them downward in a violent spiral into the ocean. Marc's arms were wrenched away from her body as they scraped against the sandy bottom. The oxygen mouthpiece flew from her mouth. She had no idea which way was up.

Tory began to panic—her lungs felt as if they would burst. Forcing her eyes open, she allowed a little precious air to escape her lips. The bubbles rose slowly past her left shoulder, and she used her last ounce of strength to follow their ascent.

As soon as her face broke the surface, she gulped air into her starving lungs. She could hear the whipping of helicopter blades. Their movement churned up the water, and white spray frothed in her face as she looked around frantically for Marc.

The pale gray of the sky blended into the dark gray ocean, making it hard to see. Swells lifted her, then dropped her down.

"Tory!" She heard Marc roar her name, and choking and gagging, she fought the tossing of the waves, her hair blinding her as it slapped across her face.

"Hold on!" He materialized behind her. She could feel the brush of his legs against hers as he trod water, holding her face above the churning sea.

Overhead, the blades of the chopper stirred up a violent wind-storm as it hovered closer to the water and lowered the rescue sling. The harness brushed the top of her head. Looking up, she saw the underside of the helicopter just thirty feet above them.

Marc snagged the harness before it sank beside her. Wedging his muscular thigh between her legs, he managed to secure the harness under her arms and keep her afloat at the same time.

She went up first. As soon as Alex had hold of Victoria, he sent the sling down for Marc. With Marc onboard, Alex slammed the door shut and made his way back to the controls up front. A few seconds later, Angelo knelt beside her, helping to support Marc as the chopper turned.

"*Buon giorno, Signorina Victoria,*" Angelo said cheerfully as his large capable hands checked Marc's forehead. "Lots of blood from a head wound, not to worry. He will have—what you say? *Il mal di testa . . .* a little headache, that is all."

Tory collapsed. Alex would get them out of here. Back home. Back to her safe, predictable life. Back to being a coward and proud of it.

So why wasn't she happy?

9

IT WAS EXACTLY SEVEN weeks, three days and five hours since the rescue. And Tory still hadn't got her life back the way it had been before Marezzo and Marc Savin. She knew she would never be the same again.

There wasn't a day that went by when she didn't think of Marc, long for him. According to Alex, Marc had recuperated and gone on another assignment.

She was all right when she went to work every day at the auto-parts store. But in the quiet times at night, alone in her rented apartment, she would think of him, dream of him, long for him.

Her breasts would ache and she would press her legs together. It took no effort at all to conjure up the memory of his callused hands. It took no effort at all to climax—alone and lonely.

Before, she'd never been lonely.

She remembered every moment with Marc and steeled her heart against the poignant memories. Her rational mind knew that it would never have worked. Because even if he'd wanted her, really wanted her, there could be no future. She couldn't live with what he did for a living. And she couldn't compete with the dead Krista's memory.

Tory came home to her quiet apartment and hung her coat in the hall closet. The living room was frigid, but she tried to keep the heat down, striving to save as quickly as possible so that she could buy another condo. Maybe when she had a real home again she would feel more settled; at least that's what she kept telling herself.

But she knew that wasn't true. She turned on some lights to dispel the gloom. Her grandmother's heavy furniture, taken out of storage, crowded the small space and suddenly she hated it. Hated the bulk and weight of the past hanging around her, suffocating her.

She vowed that as soon as she could afford to buy a home, she would get rid of all the bulky antiques and knickknacks, even if it meant sleeping on the floor. She had about six months to make it happen.

Resting her hand tenderly on her still-flat stomach, she went back to the kitchen to start dinner. She wasn't hungry, but the baby needed nourishment.

He was the best thing to come out of her adventure. Tory smiled sadly. The baby was the only thing that had prevented her from going into a dramatic Victorian decline.

Desultorily tossing a small salad and heating a can of soup, Tory took her meal back into the living room. She hadn't heard from Alex in over a month. He was off on some mission, but she hadn't felt any stirring of fear. She presumed that he was all right.

His usual letter was in the post-office box, unopened as per his instructions. She'd talked herself blue, trying to persuade him to do something else, anything else.

Perhaps, she thought without much hope, when he knew about the baby he would settle down.

Tory picked at the salad and shook her head. Alex loved what he did just as much as Marc did. Neither man would ever give up vanquishing the bad guys—not for her, and not for the baby.

So she would keep the little guy a secret as long as she could. Then she would swear Alex to secrecy. Marc must never know.

Tory was pouring the rest of the soup down the sink when she heard a knock at the door. She groaned. It was that blasted man from upstairs who was always coming over on one pretext or another. He probably wanted to borrow sugar again. He'd never gotten the clue that she wasn't interested in going out with him.

She flung open the door, her expression militant. She was going to make sure that this time her neighbor took the hint.

It wasn't her neighbor.

"I see the cast is off." Marc's pale eyes darkened as they moved across her face like a caress. "Can I come in?"

"Of . . . of course." Tory stepped back, closing the door. He was all her wildest hopes and all her dreaded fears as he scanned the overlarge furniture crowded into the small room, his eyes coming back to rest on her face. "You're looking . . . well. How are you?"

"Fine. What are you doing here?" She tugged at the hem of her lavender wool jacket. Marc saw the telltale pulse in her throat above the delicate lace collar of her cream blouse. Her hair was in a neat coil on her neck, her tiny pearl earrings rivaling the sheen of her skin.

He closed his mind to the memories that had haunted him all these weeks. He remembered painfully what her satin skin looked like under that prim little suit. He remembered with aching clarity how her magnificent hair looked loose, and how it felt like a living flame when it touched his body. His fingers twitched, and he dug them into his pockets as he remembered the sweet weight of her plump breasts in his hands.

He hadn't been able to erase the memory of her taste on his tongue or the scent of her from his mind.

He felt Victoria's eyes on his back as he moved restlessly about the room, picking up a small china dog and putting it down again. His throat felt thick as he struggled—for the first time in his life—to put what he felt into words. Words that she would understand. Words that she would believe. His fisted hands pressed back into his pockets.

Tory watched him circle the small room like a caged panther. His limp was slight, but if Tory closed her eyes for a moment she could still see what that gunshot wound had looked like. She bit the inside of her lip to keep from crying out.

His black wool overcoat was open, showing the long length of his legs, and she dragged her eyes away from the tight jeans.

Marc picked up a silver frame. "Your grandmother?"

Tory nodded. What was he doing here? Her fingers itched to touch the silky darkness of his hair where it lay against his collar. He had on a subtle, very masculine cologne; it teased her senses and made her long to bury her face against his neck.

Flicking on the lamp beside her, she sat on the overstuffed sofa, pulling a needlepoint pillow into her lap to keep her hands busy.

The soft lamplight cast half his face in shadow, hiding the pewter of his eyes and delineating the rigid line of his mouth—the mouth that had brought her so much pleasure. He looked so good, his tall body softened by the open coat. But she remembered with aching clarity the feel of his hard, hot, naked skin against hers.

The way his hands were stuffed into his front pockets pulled his jeans tight, and she had to swallow hard as she dragged her gaze upward to rest on his face.

His tanned skin in the middle of winter meant he'd been somewhere sunny. "You went back to Marezzo, didn't you?" She couldn't keep the accusatory note from creeping into her voice, her eyes skimming the small white scar on his forehead where the bullet had struck. She felt sick to her stomach.

"The job had to be finished." He circled the room again before coming to sit beside her.

She wanted to run her fingers over his body to check for any more damage. She pressed her hands between her body and the cushions on the sofa. It wasn't any of her business if he wanted to get all shot to hell. She dropped her eyes to her lap.

She started when she felt his finger under her chin. Her eyes wide, she drank in one last look at his beloved face. There were lines of strain beside his mouth, lines of exhaustion and a look of . . . longing? Which she didn't try to decipher. She closed her eyes.

"Look at me, green eyes." Tory opened her eyes reluctantly, and he filled her whole vision. More powerful than any memory. It hurt, God, how it hurt. She bit her lip. She didn't want this last look to be blurred by tears.

"God, I missed you." His tone was husky as he cupped her face. She couldn't help the way her neck seemed to lose all strength as she leaned her head against his strong hand, feeling his fingers caress her cheek one more time.

"I missed your snippy humor." His fingers slid to the lace collar at her throat. "I missed your sweet dreamy smile after we made love...." His hands opened the top two buttons of the silk blouse. Tory used a shaky hand to hold his marauding fingers still against her pounding pulse. "I missed the way this stubborn little chin tilts up...just so." His eyes were dead serious. "I missed that hidden fire that blazes out of control just for me."

"Don't," she said shakily, her heart throbbing. She knew that hot look. She'd dreamed of that look. But he wasn't for her. "Don't touch me. Please."

He didn't listen. He opened two more buttons until he got what he wanted. A vee of silky bare skin. Parting the fabric, he reverently touched the gentle swell of her breasts above her very utilitarian white cotton bra. Tory shivered.

"You love me," he said with utter conviction, his eyes on her face. She felt the blood drain from her head, leaving her weak and shaken. It was pointless trying to deny it.

"It doesn't matter." She pulled the throw pillow up against her chest, trapping his hand against her skin. "I'll get over it."

"*I* won't."

Her head shot up as she looked at him in disbelief. Surely he hadn't implied . . . ?

"I love you, Victoria Jones."

"Since when?" She tried to do up buttons but they slipped between her fingers. "Please stop. I can't think when you do that!"

He did stop, his hands rising to cup her face, his expression grave. "Since I saw a sleepy woman spitting fire at me in my library that first day. Since I tasted these sweet lips, since I touched you, since . . . forever."

"That's sex, not love."

"That's what I thought at first, too. Marry me, princess. Marry me, and I'll show you how much I love you, in so many ways. You'll forget everything else."

"I can't. I'll never be able to forget what you do for a living." Tory gave in to the temptation. She touched him back, drawing her fingers across the rough skin of his jaw to gently touch the scar on his forehead. "Every time you went away, I'd know. . . . I can't live with that. . . ." He took her hand, pressing a hard kiss into her palm. Her fingers curled inside his.

Her chest rose and fell. "I'd be terrified, especially knowing what really happens in your job when you go on an assignment. I wouldn't ask you to change for me.

And I don't think I can change enough for you." She felt the wet warmth of his tongue touch her palm.

"I'm used to being safe, I like things predictable." She tried to pull her hand away from the erotic feel of his mouth. "I don't like to take chances, Marc. It frightens me." Her eyes filled as she looked at her lap. "I'm sorry that I'm being such a wimp, but I'm too old to change now."

Marc laughed softly. "You're not a wimp and you're definitely not a coward. You are the bravest woman I know."

"No, I'm not."

"How many women do you know who would save a man's life without a second thought?" He stroked her cheek with the back of his hand. "How many women do you know who would go through what you went through and not come back a basket case?"

"How do you know I didn't?"

"Because I know you, Victoria Frances Jones. I know that you have the inner strength and the emotional fortitude to do what you have to do. You didn't fall apart." He dropped a tender kiss on her forehead. "And God only knows, you had every reason to come unglued on several occasions." His lips moved to her temple, to touch the throb of her pulse.

"Life isn't as simple as debits and credits, sweetheart. There's no neat predictability, where all the columns are totaled and neatly balanced, like your ledgers. If life was as rigid as your accounting books, we would be bored to tears."

"Bored, but safe." Victoria felt his lips skim her eyebrow. "I'd know where you were and when you'd be home."

Marc took her face between his hands. "I could get run over by a truck, Victoria. Nothing is ever totally safe."

"But the law of averages is that much higher when you're being shot at." Her voice shook and she cupped his strong hands against her cheeks, holding them there tightly. "I've always hated what Alex did, and that was just a nebulous fear. Now I *know* and it's so much worse."

"Shh." She felt his breath fan her face as he leaned down to silence her very effectively with his mouth. He tasted of mint and Marc—a flavor that she'd been yearning for for weeks. She felt his arms drawing her shoulders closer as he deepened the kiss. When he eventually broke away, he whispered against her skin, "We'll work this all out. I promise." She'd seen him furiously angry, she'd seen him playful and she'd seen him tender, but she'd never seen such seriousness in all the time that she'd known him. There was even a small spark of...what? Fear? But that was impossible. Marc had never been afraid of anything in his life. Had he?

"I had better tell you the whole story," he said. "After Krista . . . after Krista, I made myself believe that I was happier, safer alone."

"Oh, yes. Let's not forget the perfect Krista. Would you have—"

Marc gently placed a hand over her mouth. "Shh. Let me put Krista to rest once and for all. Tory, when I told you that Krista had died, I omitted to tell you one of the most salient points. I was sleeping when an assassin broke into our room. I thought that Krista was beside me and I shot to kill. But the hit 'man' was Krista. *I* was the one who shot her."

"Oh, God. Marc . . ."

"When I turned on the light and saw Krista, I convinced myself that it had been a mistake. I frantically rushed her to the hospital. She was pregnant, Tory. I—"

"Darling, don't do this to yourself. None of this matters now—"

"I went straight from Mexico to the ranch. And stayed there for two years. Alex was the one who told me that Krista had been the attempted assassin. He had proof." Marc pulled the thong out of his hair, scraping it back from his forehead with both hands. "Do you understand, Tory? I hid on my ranch for two years like some guilt-ridden fool, thinking that I had killed that innocent woman. That I had killed my child. For two goddamned years I'd allowed myself to wallow in guilt. I'd enjoyed my misery. And then your brother came and blew my life to hell with the truth. When I heard that Lynx had been killed, I really lost it. For the next six months I was worthless. I refused to go back into the field. I should have been with Lynx. I'd trained him and he had come to me for help and I had refused him. The guilt and sorrow I felt at his death incapacitated me. I fell apart. No man should collapse like a damned cream puff, but that's what I did.

"And then you came into my life and suddenly I knew that I had never loved Krista. But I wondered just what the hell I thought I could offer a woman like you. A burned-out mercenary? After I got back from Marezzo the second time and went to my ranch, I was missing you like hell and I finally realized that the solitude I had built around myself was nothing more than a jail.

"I might not deserve you, Victoria, but I sure as hell need you. Tell me you missed me half as much as I missed you."

Missed him. Yearned for him, ached for him. Her voice was whisper soft. "Yes." She looked into his eyes. "Yes, I did. I'm so sorry that you were betrayed by someone you loved. I love you more than life. I would never betray you. But I have to be honest. Your job scares me. I know what it's like when you have to dodge bullets." She touched her fingers to the scar on his forehead. "What if this had been two inches down?"

"It wasn't."

"But it could have been."

"I retired," he said roughly. "I'm just a rancher that loves you. Come back to Brandon with me, Tory. Be my love. I promise you a life filled with love and sunshine."

"I don't want to have you remind me for the rest of my life that it's because of me that you no longer do—"

"I'm not just doing this for you, green eyes. After giving it a lot of thought, I've had enough. I need to move into the light with you. I can't live without you, sweetheart. Please, say yes."

He didn't give her a chance to answer. His mouth dropped to hers in a kiss so tender and poignant that it brought tears to her eyes. The familiar taste of him made her ache.

She felt a shudder go through him as he pulled her closer, plucking the pins from her hair. His mouth moved in a slow dance across her face as his fingers threaded through her hair until it lay silky and loose down her back.

"Retired? Really?" she asked dreamily, feeling the delicious sensation as he lifted her hair at her nape.

"Really," he assured her. "I'd be thinking of you and then I'd get hard and I'd think to myself: 'Forget her.' But I never could." He smoothed the long hair over her shoulder, his eyes almost charcoal as they held the emerald of hers.

"I'm here to take you back with me. I can't live without you, Tory. Not for another day. I want you, *need* you to share all my tomorrows."

Tory stretched up to wrap her arms around his neck, his hair deliciously cool between her fingers. She felt his hand part her blouse, tugging it out of the waistband, the hand behind her neck drawing her forward. He managed to part both blouse and jacket buttons, and then his fingers were at the front clasp of her bra, and she felt the cool air on her naked breasts.

Logic deserted her, falling away as his hand skimmed her breasts, weighing, teasing until she pressed closer, her breathing forgotten.

His mouth against her throat was mobile, the hot, hard, questing pressure of his teeth making her shiver deliciously. His fingers drew the fabric aside as he moved to take one aching peak into the cavern of his mouth.

He pressed her back against the soft pillows, his hard chest pinning her in place. His fingers slid beneath the heavy fabric of her skirt, up the length of her leg, smoothing along her thigh until he came to the moist heat of her through her panty hose.

His groan was muffled by the pressure of her mouth. He traced her lips and teeth with his tongue, as his fingers slipped beneath the silky fabric to the smooth skin at her waist. Tory felt the withdrawal of her hose only dimly. Aching to be closer, she ripped at the buttons of his shirt.

Her hands were clumsy as she struggled to slide both his shirt and coat out of her way. It was impossible with their upper bodies melded together. Leaning her face against his chest, she felt his muffled, frustrated laughter.

With a low sound from the back of her throat, she lifted her face, starving for the taste of his lips again. It had been so long since she'd felt the fire of his touch. She couldn't get enough. As he loved her with his mouth, his palm covered her engorged nipple, rubbing and teasing until she shifted restlessly on the cushions. She looked up at him.

"Marc . . ."

"Tell me what you want, my love."

She saw the smoky pewter of his gaze, felt the strength in his arms as they wrapped around her. There was no doubting his love. She dropped her head to his naked chest. He smelled musky and sexy. "Anything. Everything. You," she whispered, her arms sliding up around his neck and holding him against her pounding heart.

He lifted his head, his hand cupping her stubborn little chin. "I love you more than life itself, princess. Come back to Wyoming with me. We'll raise cattle and babies...."

He buried his face into the fragrance of her hair, more afraid than he'd ever been in his life. Waiting for her answer was a thousand times worse than getting shot.

"You're mine," he said fiercely. "Do you hear me, Victoria? Mine. Tell me what you want from me, and if it's within my power I'll make sure you have it." His voice shook and he felt her arms come up to circle his shoulders.

"You," she whispered brokenly against his forehead. "Just you. Safe and whole and ... loving me. That's all I want."

"I'll give you all that and more." His mouth sealed hers with the vow. "We'll have the wedding at the ranch...."

He picked her up and carried her toward the bedroom. Tory kissed the corner of his mouth. "Yes ..."

"I have a chauffeured limo waiting downstairs and the plane is fueled and ready...."

Her lips moved to his throat. "Fine."

Marc closed his eyes, his hands stroking down her back. He said with a mock sigh, "I guess the driver can wait."

Tory looked up into warm gray eyes. "The driver can come back tomorrow."

"Maybe the day after."

"Tomorrow," she said firmly, pulling him down onto the bed with her. "I'll be temporarily done with you by then. You'll need time to recuperate for the wedding."

He didn't . . . but she did her best.

RIGHT MAN...WRONG TIME

Remember that one man who turned your world upside down? Who made you experience all the ecstatic highs of passion and lows of loss and regret. What if you met him again?

You dared to lose your heart once and had it broken. Dare you love again?

JoAnn Ross, Glenda Sanders, Rita Clay Estrada, Gina Wilkins and Carin Rafferty. Find their stories in Lost Loves, Temptation's newest miniseries, running May to September 1994.

In June, experience *WHAT MIGHT HAVE BEEN* by Glenda Sanders. Barbara had never forgotten her high school sweetheart—nor forgiven him. Richard had gotten another girl pregnant and dutifully married her. Now a single dad, he's back in town, hoping to recapture and rekindle...what might have been.

What if...?

Available in June wherever Harlequin books are sold.

Take 4 bestselling love stories FREE

Plus get a FREE surprise gift!

Special Limited-time Offer

Mail to Harlequin Reader Service®

3010 Walden Avenue
P.O. Box 1867
Buffalo, N.Y. 14269-1867

YES! Please send me 4 free Harlequin Temptation® novels and my free surprise gift. Then send me 4 brand-new novels every month, which I will receive before they appear in bookstores. Bill me at the low price of $2.44 each plus 25¢ delivery and applicable sales tax, if any.* That's the complete price and—compared to the cover prices of $2.99 each—quite a bargain! I understand that accepting the books and gift places me under no obligation ever to buy any books. I can always return a shipment and cancel at any time. Even if I never buy another book from Harlequin, the 4 free books and the surprise gift are mine to keep forever.

142 BPA AJHR

Name	(PLEASE PRINT)	
Address	Apt. No.	
City	State	Zip

This offer is limited to one order per household and not valid to present Harlequin Temptation® subscribers. *Terms and prices are subject to change without notice. Sales tax applicable in N.Y.

UTEMP-94   ©1990 Harlequin Enterprises Limited

HARLEQUIN®

Weddings, Inc.

WEDDING INVITATION
Marisa Carroll

Brent Powell is marrying Jacqui Bertrand, and the
whole town of Eternity is in on the plans. This is to be
the first wedding orchestrated by the newly formed
community co-op, Weddings, Inc., and no detail is
being overlooked.

Except perhaps a couple of trivialities. The bride is no
longer speaking to the groom, his mother is less than
thrilled with her, and her kids want nothing to do with
him.

WEDDING INVITATION, available in June
from Superromance, is the first book in Harlequin's
exciting new cross-line series, **WEDDINGS, INC.**
Be sure to look for the second book, **EXPECTA-
TIONS,** by Shannon Waverly (Harlequin Romance
#3319), coming in July.

HARLEQUIN®
Temptation®
IS TEN!

Join the festivities as Harlequin celebrates
Temptation's tenth anniversary in 1994!

Look for tempting treats from your favorite
Temptation authors all year long. The celebration
begins with Passion's Quest—four exciting sensual
stories featuring the most elemental passions....

The temptation continues with Lost Loves, a sizzling
miniseries about love lost...love found. And watch for
the 500th Temptation in July by bestselling author
Rita Clay Estrada, a seductive story in the vein
of the much-loved tale, THE IVORY KEY.

In May, look for details of an irresistible offer:
three classic Temptation novels by Rita Clay Estrada,
Glenda Sanders and Gina Wilkins in a collector's
hardcover edition—free with proof of purchase!

After ten tempting years, *nobody* can resist

Temptation®